CHOOSE YOUR OWN PATH

BIN Weevils.com

THE DREADFUL
DRAGON
DISAPPEARANCE

Other Bin Weevils books to collect:

Bin Weevils: The Official Guide (Bin-tastic Updated Edition)

Bin Weevils Puzzle Book

Bin Weevils Joke Book

Bin Weevils: Tink and Clott's Search-and-Find Adventure

Bin Weevils Doodle Storybook: Lab's Critter Contraption

Bin Weevils Sticker Activity Book

Bin Weevils Choose Your Own Path 1:
The Great Cake Disaster

Bin Weevils Choose Your Own Path 2:
The Mysterious Silence of Scribbles

Bin Weevils: The Nest Inspector's Handbook

Bin Weevils Let's Party Sticker Book

BACKWARDS BONUS!

Hold this page up to a mirror to reveal a secret code,
then enter it into the Mystery Code Machine
at Lab's Lab to unlock an exclusive nest item!

ƆTD95YAGᄃTH7

CHOOSE YOUR OWN PATH

BINWeevils.com

THE DREADFUL DRAGON DISAPPEARANCE

Written by Mandy Archer

MACMILLAN CHILDREN'S BOOKS

First published 2013 by Macmillan Children's Books
a division of Macmillan Publishers Limited
20 New Wharf Road, London N1 9RR
Basingstoke and Oxford
Associated companies throughout the world
www.panmacmillan.com

ISBN 978-1-4472-2575-1

1 3 5 7 9 8 6 4 2

A CIP catalogue record for this book is available from
the British Library.

Printed and bound by CPI Group (UK) Ltd, Croydon CR0 4YY

Ker-ching!

It's not even lunchtime, but you can tell it's going to be an awesome day in the Bin. You've just withdrawn your salary from the cash machine and you're ready to flip out! For months now you've been admiring the stunning crown on display in Hem's hat-shop window. The diamond creation is worthy of true Bin Royalty! It's taken a whole lot of scrimping and saving, but business is going well and you've finally stockpiled enough Dosh to buy it!

Now you and your loyal buddy Clott are on your way to the Shopping Mall to collect Tink from the Garden Shop. Tink has been helping Tab out, sweeping the floor and stacking up plant pots. As soon as he clocks off, the three of you are going to Tycoon Plaza to purchase your lovely new crown. Then it's off to Rigg's Multiplex to catch a movie before a slap-up meal at Figg's Cafe. Bin-tastic!

'Morning, Tab!' you bellow, throwing the door open so enthusiastically it nearly comes off its hinges.

The poor shopkeeper leaps up in surprise, whacking his antennae on the ceiling! Clott makes things worse by accidentally kicking a stack of flowerpots across the floor.

'Careful!' screeches Tab, frantically fanning himself with an empty seed packet. The green-thumbed Bin Weevil always looks worried, but today he seems Freaked with a capital 'F'! It's hardly surprising, as there's a crowd of customers swarming all over the shop.

'Can't talk, I'm afraid,' he shrugs. 'Bonkers busy right now!'

'We're not here to buy anything,' you explain.

'We just need Tink,' pipes up Clott.

Tab hasn't got time to listen. He's bagging up a Pit of Mystery plant for a busy-looking grey Bin Weevil. You and Clott shuffle your way to the back of the queue.

At the counter Twigg is studying a rare Angler Orchid seed under his magnifying glass, while Posh is moaning loudly that she should have sent the family butler Bosh along to do her queuing for her. As for Tink, he's dangling from a shelf trying to reach a row of blue picket fencing that Glum has got his eye on. You give your pal an excited wave, but he shrugs his shoulders – there's no way he can leave poor Tab on his own in the store right now.

'What about Hem's?' you worry. If anyone else snaps up that diamond crown, it would be a total travesty!

Clott doesn't reply. Instead he straightens his top hat, slicks down his eyebrows and grins daftly in a certain direction. Of course! The preening is all for Posh's benefit – Clott has been trying to impress her since . . . forever!

You sigh, then do what any honourable Bin Weevil would do – dig deep, muck in and help out.

You're just serving Posh when Trigg bursts into the shop and barges up to the counter, exclaiming he needs a Leopard Chilli Vine super-urgently! The hubbub in the Garden Shop drops to a hush. Nine nosy Bin Weevils crane their necks. What is going on? The SWS agent is known for many things, but his love of spicy plants isn't one of them!

'Doing a spot of gardening, eh?' you say casually.

'That information is classified,' replies Trigg. As a respected SWS agent, he gives nothing away.

'Of course,' you assure him, before adding, 'You couldn't give us even a teensy tiny clue then?'

'We'll say "pretty, pretty please"!' pleads Tink, before jumping into Trigg's outstretched arms.

Everyone in the shop takes a step closer, their antennae pricked up. Trigg releases Tink and sighs. All he *will* say is

that he's out running an errand for Gam, the chief of the

service. He presses a wad of Mulch into your hand, grabs the Leopard Chilli packet and scuttles out the door before Posh and co. can utter a word.

It's only when you're putting the Mulch in Tab's cash register that you spot Trigg has given you twice the amount of money shown on the price tag. No SWS agent worth his badge would make a mistake like that, *unless it was on purpose*!

You give Tink and Clott a knowing wink and cock your head towards the door. The duo stare back blankly. Doh! Your pals are knockout SWS agents, but they're not the quickest brains in the Binscape sometimes!

'Hate to bail, Tab,' you call, 'but something weevily urgent has come up. Laters, everyone!'

You bustle out of the shop, dragging Tink and Clott with you. As predicted, Trigg is waiting for you. He signals to follow him. One by one, you creep out of the Shopping Mall and dart behind a giant billboard.

Muttering under his breath and with eyes scanning in all directions, Trigg reveals grave news – there has been a suspected Bin-nap! You gulp as Trigg recounts that Gam's beloved pet dragon Colin has gone missing!

'The boss was out for walkies with Colin when the unthinkable happened,' says Trigg. 'Colin trotted off to fetch a stick and never came back!'

Tink and Clott's mouths drop. Gam has had Colin ever since he discovered a precious cracked rainbow egg as a young Bin Weevil, m-a-n-y years ago. Although he has a tail that could flatten Flum's Fountain in one swish and enough firepower to barbecue a thousand Bin Burgers, Colin is devoted to his miniature master.

'How could someone steal him away?' you ask. 'Colin is over eleven Bin Nests tall!'

3

Trigg's mouth narrows. 'Sinister forces may be at work,' he says seriously. 'We cannot rule out the WEB's involvement.'

The WEB is the evil organization led by Octeelia, the arch-enemy of the Secret Weevil Service. The scheming spider is always trying to stir up trouble in the Binscape, but swiping Colin would be an all-time low!

Trigg points at each of you – he needs you to join the hunt for Colin. Fellow agent, Kong Fu, is searching the Castle dungeons and Fink is doing some undercover investigations around Tycoon Island. Gam, meanwhile, is stationed at the mission control room. The priority is to find Colin before word gets out that the WEB are back. Bin Weevils will soon start to panic!

Clott's bottom lip begins to tremble. 'This mission sounds a bit dangerous!'

Tink fiddles furiously with an imaginary watch. 'The film starts at five,' he witters. 'Mustn't be late . . .'

You look at your buddies and sigh. An afternoon at the movies would have been nice, but you've got a job to do. Colin needs to be found – and fast!

'Come on, boys!' you reply, racking your Bin-brain for ideas. 'Trigg needs us. Now . . . where to find a runaway dragon?'

It's up to you to think sharp and make some weevily smart choices. Colin's fiery future is in your hands!

If you decide to start with a trip to the Bin Pet Shop, go to page 31.

If you'd rather kick off the search in the dank dungeons of Castle Gam, go to page 51.

You promise Gam that you'll find his dear dragon before supper, and then scurry over to Flum's Fountain. By the time you skid across the gravel, the place is packed. Bin Weevils mooch around in circles, chatting to their friends and catching up on all the latest gossip. You spot Scribbles brandishing the latest edition of *Weevil Weekly* and the Nest Inspector comparing Bin-terior decorating notes with his old friend, Fab.

'There's Bunty,' whispers Tink. 'Duck!'

You spot the Bin's busiest Bin Weevil standing next to the fountain, talking nineteen to the dozen. Bunty is a great pal, but not one to bump into when you're in a hurry. If there's any gossip going round the Binscape, Bunty is bound to know about it. In fact, the chances are that she started it in the first place! You decide to keep a low profile. If you get caught nattering with Bunty, you're unlikely to track down Colin any time this side of Christmas.

You and your Bin buddies bundle behind a stone pillar and crash straight into Hunt! The puzzle genius is kneeling on all sixes, studying a patch of ground through her magnifying glass. It seems that she has turned up to do some sleuthing of her own.

'I was having an early morning stroll when I heard about Colin,' she explains. 'I decided to hang around and make myself useful.'

Hunt points to a set of dragon footprints that trails off into the distance. The tracks seem to be leading towards Flem Manor – or could it be Club Fling?

If you choose to head to Flem Manor, go to page 80.
If you decide to check out Club Fling first, go to page 84.

5

'Every Bin Weevil for themselves!' you cry, collapsing into a commando roll and tumbling back down the tunnel.

Your new plan is a no-brainer – when a Bin Weevil's eyebrows start to singe it's definitely time to get out of the dungeon! Tink, Clott, Flem and even Kong Fu are all right behind you, scurrying just out of reach of the flames. It's only when poor Flem has to stop for a sneezing fit that the heat finally catches up with you.

'Well, well, well . . . !' cackles a horribly familiar voice.

You turn round and are confronted by Octeelia, riding on Colin's back! The distressed dragon has a chain round his neck and manacles fixed around his ankles. Octeelia's drone-like Thuggs stand on either side, ready to restrain the reptile should he attempt to break free. As soon as Colin spots your friendly faces, he sniffs to put out his fire.

'Don't stop the flames!' shrieks Octeelia, pulling on the chains. The dragon courageously ignores the command, even when his captor uses each of her eight pointed feet to dig into his neck.

'Let Colin go!' you cry.

Octeelia sneers at her henchmen, then bursts into hysterical laughter.

'Colin's mine now,' she glares. 'Don't worry, I won't steal him. You'll get a fair swap.'

You watch aghast as the arachnid claps her hands. You're suddenly aware of another enormous shape filling up the shadowy dungeon. A second dragon appears in the tunnel – a second dragon that is the spitting image of Colin! You eye him up and down suspiciously. Apart from a tiny purple scale at the end of his tail, it's impossible to tell the creatures apart.

'Meet Rupert,' sighs Octeelia. 'Colin's long-lost twin!'

'Huh?' the Bin Weevils in the tunnel all gasp at once.

You remember Gam telling tales by firelight of Colin's long-lost brother, but you never believed that they were any more than fairy stories. The yarn went back to the days of the Great Bin War! Gam had saved Colin before he'd even hatched out of his egg, but his brother had not been so lucky. Over the years, Rupert's fortunes went from bad to worse, with the dragon ending up in the hands of Octeelia and her underlings. You peer into Rupert's eyes, expecting to see cruelty and menace. To your surprise, the creature gives you a friendly wink. It's only then that you realize that this poor dragon is in chains too.

'Why, you wicked . . .' shouts Kong Fu, throwing a perfect roundhouse kick in Octeelia's general direction.

The evil mastermind is one step ahead. Quick as a flash, she yanks Rupert's chain and tugs it towards the SWS agent.

'Barbecue that bug!' she roars. 'Turn him into toast!'

You wince as Rupert opens his ferocious jaws and bares his teeth. You, Tink and Clott wait for the fireball that will inevitably follow. To your astonishment, nothing happens. Instead, the shame-faced dragon can only muster a feeble yelp. You're shocked – you've got cuddly toys in your nest back home that squeak more loudly than that!

'Oh, forget it!' barks Octeelia. 'Totally pathetic! You're

never going to learn how to breathe fire, even after a decade at dragon school!'

Poor Rupert hangs his head in shame. Now you're on to the WEB's game – Octeelia has snatched Gam's scaly pal so he can teach her pet dragon to breathe fire! It looks like Rupert is a slow learner, but you know never to underestimate Octeelia. If Rupert won't heat things up, there's nothing to stop the wicked leader keeping Colin instead!

You are the only Bin Weevils with the slightest chance of foiling Octeelia's plans. How are you going to drive the nasty spider and her hundred horrid henchmen out? All you have in your arsenal are a pocket full of Dosh and four determined helpers.

If you're willing to distract Octeelia so Colin can be freed, go to page 10.
If you'd prefer to buy your way out of trouble, go to page 83.

'Let's go, Agents!'

You career towards the Track Builder garage as fast as your legs will carry you. A fire in the garage would be a mega-disaster – the place is packed full of petrol cans, tyres and other Bin-tastically burnable driving gear!

You skid into the workshop and discover . . . Colin lying on his back blowing smoke rings in the air!

'Hic!'

Every so often the dragon is racked with a hiccup that turns the smoke into a billowing burst of flame.

'Calm down, Colin,' you say gently. 'Go easy with the fire breathing. It's fine in the dungeons, but not quite so clever out here in Dirt Valley.'

As soon as he sees you, the delighted dragon leaps to his feet and trots over, knocking you upside down. You pick yourself up, hoping that the beast won't hiccup again any time soon.

'What are you doing here?' asks Clott, reaching up to give the dragon a scratch at the base of his ear.

Colin pulls back, ashamed.

'Have you been exploring again?' scolds Tink. 'Gam was worried about you!'

The dragon nods his head slowly, then blows a series of the tiniest smoke rings to say sorry. It's hard to stay cross with a cutie like a Colin! It's been a crazy day, but all's well that ends well. You've cracked your mission and there's still time for tea at Tum's Diner!

The End

You sneak another peek at Rupert. The crestfallen dragon turns his head away, but not before you notice a large teardrop plop to the ground. It's stonkingly obvious that the creature doesn't have an evil bone in his body! You also have a hunch that he might just hold the key to cracking this messy mission.

'Let's split,' shrieks Octeelia, tugging on her new servant's chains. 'It's time we left these losers alone.'

Colin suddenly swipes his claws and flicks his tail hard. He's determined to stay put.

'Watch out!' shouts Clott, as a legion of Thuggs all jab and prod at the poor creature, forcing him back towards the wall. Gam's dragon is majorly outnumbered!

You take one last glimpse at Rupert, then step out from the shadows. You secretly signal for your pals to come forward too.

'Is that the best you can do?' you mock, pulling a face at Octeelia's lackeys. 'Pathetic!'

The Thuggs begin to mutter and glare.

'What a bunch of weaklings!' agrees Tink, poking out his tongue. 'I've met tougher Bin Pet groomers!'

Flem backs

you up by blowing a massive raspberry through his snotty handkerchief.

Octeelia's eyes narrow. You and Clott gulp. You've both got a funny feeling that you're going to like her even less when she's angry.

'Get them!' she screams, sending the Thuggs over to inflict the worst punishment they can muster.

You and your Bin Buddies have your backs against the wall, but you can't help smiling secretly to yourself. Kong Fu does such a cracking job of karate-chopping the Thuggs, the baddies don't notice Rupert sidling up beside his twin.

In the blink of an eye, Colin uses his fire to melt his brother's chains. Rupert returns the favour by gnawing through Colin's manacles.

'Aaaggghh!'

You all cheer as Colin throws Octeelia from his back. Funnily enough, the Thuggs don't hang around long enough to see what treats the dragons have got in store for them. As they run screaming out of the dungeons you make your way upstairs to tell Gam the good news. Excellent work, Agent!

The End

You really want to scarper, but you have to do the right thing. You form a Bin Weevil tower and carefully lift a flaming torch from the wall and hand it to Flem.

'Head to the mission control room! This could get ugly . . .'

Tink raises an arm. 'Permission to escort Flem back to safety?' he says sheepishly.

'Permission to help Tink escort Flem to safety?' adds Clott.

'I'm afraid not, Agents,' you sigh. 'We've work to do.'

As Flem scuttles away, you and your buddies surge forward together. The tunnel narrows before stopping in front of a slimy stone wall.

'Looks like the only way is up,' mutters Clott.

He's right – his top hat is hooked on to a rusty ladder bolted halfway up the wall! One by one, you clamber up. Some rungs are slippery and others have rotted away altogether. You keep climbing until daylight appears.

'Creeping compost!'

You stick your head out of the hole and blink in the afternoon sun. The tunnel has surfaced in the slime-splattered grounds of Castle Gam. Astonishing! But what's even more eye-popping is that you can see not one but *two* identical dragons. One is circling above the battlements, while the other is aiming fireballs at Octeelia and her cronies.

'We've found Colin!' you shout, pulling Tink and Clott up behind you.

Tink scratches his head. 'Er, which one is he?'

> If you think you should try to leap on to the dragon
>   in the sky, go to page 24.
> If you've got your sights set on the fire-breather
>   instead, go to page 62.

'Hold your horses, chaps,' you urge. 'Let's give this some thought. What's the best thing about Flum's Fountain?'

'Ooh, I know!' cries Clott, sticking his hand in the air. 'It's the jets on the fountain. Got to be the best way to water mushrooms.'

'No,' argues Tink. 'It's all the cool Bin Weevils you get to meet pounding the paths.'

You tap your foot impatiently as your buddies launch into a heated debate. The daft doughnuts have forgotten the best feature of all – the Free Cam that lets you take pics and video of everything that's going on in and around the fountain.

'Gam,' you ask. 'Can you access the Free Cam from here?'

The SWS leader flips open a hidden panel on the table and punches in a key code. Suddenly a view of Flum's Fountain is projected into the air above his desk!

'Wind back a few hours,' you instruct, scanning the picture for clues.

You can't help giggling as Gam scrolls back the tape – watching busy Bin Tycoons tootling along backwards around the fountain makes for amusing viewing! When the soldier sees you sniggering, you take care to pull yourself together and sit up straight.

'There you are, sir!' cries Clott, pointing to a bent-over figure following a hulking great dragon.

You all watch in silence as Gam potters up and down the path, throwing a stick to his over-excited pal. He hurls the stick into the grass, then perches on the side of the fountain while Colin bounds off to fetch it. You note that Dosh, Bunty and the Garden Inspector stop by to say hello. You even see Tum wave good morning as she heads off to work at the Diner. For a while the path clears, save for one or two

Bin Weevils scurrying in and out of the frame.

'Stop the tape!' you suddenly cry.

You point to a shady figure wearing a white peaked hat. The Bin Weevil is clutching something to her chest and scampering shiftily along the wall.

'Who is that?' you ask. 'I've never seen *her* before.'

The SWS leader falls silent.

'Gam?' asks Tink. 'Do you know that Bin Weevil?'

Clott leaps out of his seat. 'Come on, boss! You can't keep a secret from a secret agent!'

It takes a lot more nagging for Gam to admit that he knows exactly who the Bin Weevil is. It's Sink, a submarine captain who's been working for the Secret Weevil Service for years.

'I trust Sink with my most secret secrets,' he confesses. 'She keeps them on board her sub, in the deepest depths of the ocean outside Mulch Island.'

'Think hard,' you say seriously. 'Could Sink be hiding anything to do with Colin?'

Gam's face breaks into a grimace. He slowly nods his head.

'Sink knows everything about Colin's past. Everything!'

If you think it's time to head out to Mulch Island and track down Sink, go to page 47.

If you want to watch the Free Cam one more time, go to page 87.

Your brain is panicking, but there are a few horrible milliseconds before the message reaches your legs. By the time you turn and run, the dragon is already brandishing a toothy grin! Tink, Clott and Hunt are scrabbling away, just a stone's throw ahead of you.

'Head for that shrub!' you bellow.

One by one, you dive behind the only protection for miles around – a rather pathetic-looking patch of Elephant Grass. The dragon pounds up to the grass, opens his jaws and prepares to unleash . . .

. . . a rather squeaky hiccup!

'What was that?' asks Tink, poking his head out in surprise.

'I was expecting my top hat to be toast by now!' guffaws Clott.

You grin at your pals. It seems that this dragon can't breathe fire! Suddenly he's not quite so scary. You step out of the grass and gingerly step forward. To your delight, the beast doesn't decide to gobble you up.

'Tink! Clott! Can you run and fetch Gam?' you ask. 'I think he might like to meet our new friend.'

Your mates tear back to Castle Gam, leaving you and Hunt to dragon-sit. By the time the SWS leader finally arrives, the creature is making happy

Castle Gam

little squeaks as you scamper up and down the bony plates on his tail. Who would have thought dragons were ticklish?

Gam stares at the dragon in disbelief for a full five minutes.

'Rupert?' he says tentatively. 'Can that really be you?'

At the sound of his name, the creature stamps his feet with such excitement that you have to cling on to each other to steady yourselves. Gam hugs the delighted dragon.

'Let me introduce Colin's twin brother,' he announces proudly. 'Colin and Rupert were separated years ago, before they'd even had the chance to hatch out of their eggs. The last I heard, this poor beast was in the gruesome grip of the WEB.'

You frown knowingly at Tink and Clott. Trust the Weevil Extermination Bureau to cause trouble in the Bin!

'He must have escaped,' you decide, giving Rupert a kindly pat.

The dragon nods his head. It was almost as if he understood exactly what you were saying!

'Now we have a real mystery on our hands,' says Hunt excitedly. 'These stones are covered in burn marks, yet Colin is still missing. We know that Rupert can't breathe fire, so Colin must have been here earlier today. The question is . . . where is he now?'

You all stand in a flummoxed silence for a moment, until you have a brainwave.

'Let's ask Rupert,' you suggest. 'I bet he knows!'

You gasp in surprise as the dragon carefully uses his tail to scoop you all up on to his back. Before long you find yourselves soaring over the Binscape! Rupert lands in a deserted glade not far from Tink's Tree. There, deep in the forest, is a secret dragon's lair lined with mushrooms and

Scent Flowers. The air hangs thick with the heady scent of over-ripe fruit.

'Colin!'

Gam's pal appears from the lair, and rushes up to greet his master with a curious bleat. Suddenly, everything falls into place. After meeting his long-lost brother at Flum's Fountain, Colin has taken some time out to find a hiding spot for Rupert far away from Octeelia and her Thuggs.

Gam is over the moon.

'So that's why you disappeared!' chuckles the old soldier, pulling a magic bean out of his pocket and aiming it at Colin's mouth. 'Rupert can't hide out here, though, he'll be much safer staying in the castle dungeons with me!'

You, Tink and Clott give each other a proud high-five. You're not sure quite how you've done it, but you've come out of this mission with flying colours. Gam only lost one dragon, but you managed to find him two!

The End

The helicopter door appears to be jammed – whoever is inside has even started kicking and banging on the windows! You, Tink and Clott run up to the chopper, grab the handle and tug . . .

Bop!

A spindly figure comes flying out of the cockpit so fast that she lands head first in the Information Booth opposite! You rush over and pull the creature's legs out again, setting her straight on the tarmac.

'Get off me!' barks the bug, slapping you away.

You all spring back in surprise. Octeelia is standing before you, her face creased into an ugly frown.

'Ugh!' wails Tink, reeling from the shock. 'I cannot believe I just helped the head of the WEB! I shall forever be ashamed!'

For a moment you are lost for words. Octeelia is the mastermind behind the evil Weevil Extermination Bureau. The vile villain has made it her mission to get control of the Binscape. She never surfaces unless there's some serious trouble afoot. The horrible sinking feeling in the pit of your tummy tells you that the latest bout of serious trouble must have something to do with Colin.

'What do you want?' you shout bravely. 'I suppose you've come here to cause chaos and destruction!'

Octeelia scowls horribly. 'Of course I have!' she snarls. 'And if it hadn't been for this wretched reptile I would have done it too.'

The arachnid angrily smacks her fist three times on the side of the helicopter.

'Weevil X!' she orders. 'Release the captive!'

The helicopter door sticks and shakes once more, until it finally creaks open. You make a mental note to remind Dosh to buy some oil when he next pops by.

'Colin!'

You watch, dumbfounded, as poor Colin bundles his bulky body through the tiny helicopter passenger door. He lands on the ground with a resounding crash. Wowee! You knew that dragons were magical but that spectacle defied science!

The dragon looks bewildered and somewhat squished, but is basically A-OK. You run over and pat his left nostril gently.

'Ew! Don't give him any affection! He's utterly useless!' Octeelia grimaces.

'What's wrong with him?' you demand.

'What's the use of a dragon that can't fly? I've already got one useless creature in my power, I certainly don't want two,' she sneers.

With that, the super-baddy clicks her fingers. An eerie squeak rings out from the apartment block opposite. Suddenly another dragon leaps from the helipad and soars into the skies. The creature is a dead-ringer for Colin – they could even be long-lost twins.

That's when the penny drops. They *are* long-lost twins! You remember Gam telling you stories of how he first came across Colin's egg all those years ago. There had been another identical dragon baby, but it had fallen into the wrong hands.

'Rupert!' shrieks Octeelia, clicking her fingers.

The dragon obediently glides to the ground, taking his place beside Colin. There's nothing to pick the pair apart, save for a tiny purple scale on Rupert's tail. Octeelia prods him meanly in the eye.

'This one can't breathe fire,' she snaps, 'so I thought I'd steal the SWS's dragon instead. I could do serious damage with a creature like that! Nobody told me that Colin couldn't fly! We had to pinch Dosh's helicopter just to transport him away from Flum's Fountain. Complete waste of time! Have you ever travelled in a helicopter with a fully grown dragon? It's murder!'

Octeelia's rant goes on and on until Weevil X jumps out of the helicopter and drags her away by the arm.

'Let's go,' he urges. 'This place is crawling with Bin Weevils.'

'Fine!' she snaps. 'You can keep Colin and you can keep Rupert too. Next time I do something it will be r-e-a-l-l-y bad and I won't need anyone's help!'

You all cheer as the failed nasties scuttle out of sight. This mission seems to have solved itself, but what does that matter? The important thing is that Colin will soon be back where he belongs. And with a new best buddy in Rupert, he'll never be short of a playmate.

'Righto!' you grin. 'Who's coming with me to Hem's Hats? Maybe there's a sale on.'

The End

You dance through the palm trees, then shimmy over to the Smoothie Shack and pull up a stool. It's one cool place — from here you can see across the whole of the Slime Pool, while slurping an ice-cold drink.

Sip appears from behind the bar and passes you a menu. Sip is always thirsty, so it's a good thing that she's also the Shack's owner! Whenever the Bin Weevil's at work she likes to dress up in flower garlands and hula skirts. She says it's to get her customers in the party mood, but she doesn't seem in the mood to party right now. While you chat, she stands at the back of the Shack washing up glasses.

'Maybe she's just having an off-day?' shrugs Tink, choosing a Lime Slime.

Clott decides on a Groovy Smoothie, but you just can't make up your mind. Last time you were here you're sure you had a smoothie flavoured with sweaty sock, but you really can't remember its name. There's a new drink on the list today, however. Sip has written ICE SLOSHY in big blue letters.

'Can I have one of those?' you ask. 'A Sloshy sounds very refreshing!'

Sip shakes her head sadly and turns away.

'All out of Sloshy, I'm afraid,' she mutters. 'Why don't you stick to an Awesome Poursome?'

You shoot a glance at Tink and Clott. Sip really isn't her jolly self today. You ponder why that could be. You also can't help wondering how she managed to run out of Sloshy before lunchtime!

You're just about to quiz Sip a little more when there's a loud rustling in the bushes. Before you can say 'Make mine a Peach on the Beach', your hostess ducks behind the Shack counter, hiding herself from view.

If you want to ask Sip some probing questions, go to page 42.

If you decide to check out the weird rustling noise, go to page 75.

Secretly you'd love to nab a signed photo of Ham for your nest, but you can't let Colin down in his hour of need. You decide to play it super-cool, hoping to persuade your friends to stick to the mission in hand.

'Let's do some sleuthing over by the flagpoles,' you wink. 'I wouldn't be surprised if Ham wanted to wander over and see *us*. We are highly trained SWS agents, after all.'

Clott and Tink fall for it hook, line and sinker, trotting along behind you. Soon, the three of you are snooping through the grass around the charred flagpoles, hunting for clues. Luckily your efforts are rewarded – the mud is lumped and bumped with trails of dragon footprints!

'Colin's been here!' thunders Tink, jumping into Clott's arms. 'Go us!'

'He's *still* here, in fact,' chips in a helpful voice. 'Shall I take you to see him?'

You turn on your heels to see Ham himself, grinning! Clott and Tink are dumbstruck – Ham is a legend in the Binscape! No one can race faster than him. You don't know what's more thrilling: being this close to your hero or finding out that Colin's safe.

Whoosh!

You are just about to take Ham up on his offer when a ball of flame billows out from the Track Builder garage. Dirt Valley is on fire!

If you have got the courage to check out the fire in the garage, go to page 9.
If you choose to seek out Colin first, go to page 76.

'Let's try that Bin Weevil tower again!' shouts Clott, scrambling to his feet.

You struggle on to Clott's shoulders, then reach down and yank Tink on to yours. Clott staggers towards the flying dragon, groaning under your combined weevily weight.

'Do what you gotta do!' he bellows. 'But please, make it quick!'

Your tower wobbles left and right, as the dragon swoops round and round above your head, snapping his jaws and flicking his scarlet tail. Tink stretches his arms as far as he can and makes a lunge for a spine on the creature's back.

Oomph!

Unfortunately he misses. The three of you land on the ground with a wallop-tastic thud.

'Now what?' you wonder, watching the dragon launch itself even higher in the sky. The ferocious creature circles the stronghold's grey turrets, eyeing you suspiciously.

At that moment, Gam ambles along the drawbridge, walking stick in hand. As the oldest Bin Weevil in the Bin, he's seen more than his fair share of drama. You've lost count of the nights he's sat regaling you with tales from his glory days. Even so, the bedlam before him seems to take the biscuit. Gam's jaw drops so low, his false gnashers almost fall out!

'Octeelia's got Colin!' you explain. 'Look, up there!'

Gam pulls off his helmet, his face aghast. It takes the flustered old soldier a full five minutes to explain that the creature in the sky cannot be Colin. His beloved pal is totally terrified of flying!

You gulp. Colin must be the fire-breathing creature doing battle with Octeelia and her evil weevils!

How can the real Colin be rescued? Go to page 28 to find out!

'OK,' you agree. 'I guess we should check in with Gam first. There might have been some new developments that we agents need to know about.'

Tink and Clott nod enthusiastically, then scamper after you. Your heart thumps in your chest as you stride over the drawbridge into the castle. There are lots of places in the 'Scape where an animal could get lost, but Colin isn't like most of the critters round here – the ginormous dragon is at least 18,000 times bigger! How could he disappear without a single Bin Weevil noticing?

You hastily turn the bar to open the vaulted door to the SWS mission control room, then wait for the laser detection system to approve your ID. Within moments you find yourselves standing in a high-tech operations room surrounded by computer screens, flashing lights and important-looking switches.

'Remember,' you hiss to Tink and Clott. 'Don't. Touch. ANYTHING.'

Clott runs a finger over a big red button marked with the words 'FOR EMERGENCY USE ONLY'.

'Can I just see what this one does?' he asks innocently.

'Noooo!'

Gam shuffles into the mission control room, furiously waving his walking stick at Clott. You notice that all the other operatives around you have thrown themselves to the floor.

'If you press that,' he booms, 'every nest in the Binscape will be buried in compost!'

Clott shuffles away from the control desk, but not before shooting you a look that says 'Hmm . . . let's try that later!'

Gam beckons to you to sit down. The soldier has been an old-timer ever since you can remember, but today he looks positively ancient. The loss of his darling dragon is

25

already taking its toll on the chief of the SWS, it seems. Gam has cared for Colin ever since he first discovered his rainbow egg back in the days of the Great Bin War. He even named the critter after his great-great-grandfather, Gam Colin IV.

Tink slips on his secret agent shades, then pulls a notebook from his pocket.

'We'll help you, sir,' he says kindly. 'Can you talk us through exactly what happened?'

A large salty tear brims in Gam's eye.

'It was a normal morning,' he explains. 'I was taking Colin for his daily walkies round Flum's Fountain. We like to go early, when the place is quiet. I sat down on the edge of the fountain to watch Colin make mush of the mushrooms. After five or ten minutes, Colin brought me a stick just like he always does. I threw it into the grass and he scampered off to fetch it. I stopped to say hello to a couple of passing Bin Tycoons, then ambled over to see what Colin was up to. I called and called, but he was . . . gone!'

You pass the old soldier a hankie, turning away discreetly while he noisily blows his nose.

'Was there anyone strange hanging around?' asks Clott.

Gam sniffs loudly, then taps his helmet.

'The old memory's not as sharp as it used to be, lads,'

he admits. 'I can't remember anyone in particular. I can only assume the worst.'

'What's that?' asks Tink, puzzled.

'That someone r-e-a-l-l-y sneaky staked out the Fountain, then stole Colin from under my nose,' replies Gam. 'All the signs point to the WEB – they're the only outfit sly enough to pull off an operation like that.'

A shiver shudders from the top of your antennae right down to your toes. An uncomfortable question pops into your head. If Octeelia and her crew have got their claws into Colin, what are they going to do with him now?

'I vote that we skedaddle over to Flum's Fountain straight away,' blurts out Clott.

Tink furiously nods his head.

If you are ready to check out the Fountain, go to page 5.

If you'd rather quiz Gam for more information, go to page 13.

You dash across the castle grounds, ducking and diving to avoid the flying dragon's claws. The impostor swoops above your heads, its eyes flashing with fury.

'Who rattled his cage?' blurts out Tink, ducking behind an empty Konnect Mulch playboard. Clott skids in behind him, closely followed by a very nervous-looking Flem.

'I couldn't get to the mission control room,' he splutters. 'Those dungeons are full of dead-ends and blind alleys. Sniff!'

'Don't worry,' you reply, 'I think Gam's got the message.'

You poke your head above the playboard and point to the SWS leader. The senior Bin Weevil is peeping out from behind a slime cauldron, waving his stick furiously at Octeelia and her henchmen.

If there were other Bin Weevils around, they have had the good sense to scarper out of sight. You can't blame them – a band of Thuggs doing battle against two agitated dragons is likely to spell disaster, any which way you look at it!

Your heart thumps and your palms sweat. All six of your legs are shaking. This is an emergency!

'When I say "Run, Bin Weevil, run!", make a dash for Gam,' you order, hoping the soldier will have some ideas on how to get Octeelia and her crew out of the Binscape.

Clott's eyebrows start to knot.

'Erm, was that "*One* Bin Weevil, run!" or "*Run*, Bin Weevil, run!"?' he asks earnestly.

'Can't afford to get it wrong, boss,' Tink helpfully pipes up.

'Just follow me!' you bark, scrambling to your feet.

You, Tink, Clott and Flem pick your way across the castle grounds, ducking to avoid the strange red dragon terrorizing the skies above you. You can't understand it – the bogus beast *looks* just the same as Colin, but it seems to be in a seriously bad mood. Again and again it loops down over your heads, swiping at you and snapping its teeth. You're lucky to reach Gam in one piece.

'We've got to help Colin,' he mutters. 'The WEB have got him surrounded.'

You nod your head, but point up to the hostile dragon soaring over the castle.

'I think that fella might have something to say about it,' you reply.

Gam shakes his head, then breaks into a toothy grin.

'Don't worry about him,' he says. 'Now let me tell you a story . . .'

You can't quite believe your ears. Is right now *really* the right time for another of Gam's endless yarns? Colin is in danger! You try to get to your feet, but the old Bin Weevil grabs you by the collar.

Gam explains breathlessly that the dragon flying above your heads isn't an evil WEB servant, but Colin's long-lost twin brother, Rupert! The only difference between the dragons is a tiny purple scale that flashes at the end of Rupert's tail. The pair hatched from matching rainbow eggs, back in the days of the Great Bin War. While Gam managed to rescue Colin from cruel enemy hands, Rupert ended up in the clutches of Octeelia and her mob.

'So what are they doing here?' asks Tink.

The SWS agent's question is interrupted by a cackle more screeching than nails on a blackboard. Octeelia herself has scuttled over to join in the conversation! You shudder – the awful arachnid has never been this close before. Her spindly legs, lipsticked sneer and fluttering eyelashes ooze horribleness from every pore.

'My dragon is useless,' she smirks, 'so I've come to seize yours! Colin can breathe fire. When Rupert roars, he's lucky to produce a puff of smoke! There's not a drop of evil in his body. That's why I hatched a plan to use Rupert to lure Colin away from you. And rather brilliant it was too . . .'

'Tell me more,' you say enthusiastically.

Your friends think you're Bin-bonkers, but a secret wink keeps them quiet. All evil masterminds love bragging about how smart they are, and Octeelia is no exception. While she loses herself in the sound of her own voice, two cheesed-off dragons silently creep up behind her.

'Yooowwwwl!'

Suddenly Rupert swoops in, swiping Octeelia in his claws. Colin leaps forward and growls, producing a fiery flame ball. Terrified Thuggs scurry in every direction.

Tink and Clott give you an impressed hug. The dragon is just a small dot in the distance when you hear a final, ear-splitting scream.

'Oops!' chuckles Gam, 'Rupert must have dropped her.'

The End

You say your goodbyes to Trigg, then dive back into the Shopping Mall. As you wander past shop windows looking for inspiration, you examine the facts one more time.

'Was Colin Bin-napped,' you wonder, 'or did he run away?'

'Bin-napped for sure!' insists Clott.

'Colin loved Gam,' reasons Tink. 'Why run away from his best pal?'

You have to agree. Gam has looked after Colin for more years than you care to remember. He even named the beloved dragon after his great-great-grandfather, Gam Colin IV! You and your mates are still considering the options when a Bin Weevil peeps her head out of a store and calls your name.

'Hi! Coming in, then?'

It's Dott, the owner of the Bin Pet Shop. Not only is Dott the friendliest Bin Weevil in town, she's also an expert Bin Pet trainer. She thinks all critters are cute and cuddly – even the naughty ones! He's not your average Bin Pet, but if anybody would know how to try to track down Colin, it would be Dott. You scuttle in to say hello.

The store is buzzing this morning. Adorable Bin Pets bounce around in the playpen while excited Bin Tycoons queue up to buy food bowls, pet food and juggling balls. Posh has trip-trapped in from the Garden Shop next door, holding her own pink princess, Lady Wawa. Posh and her pampered Bin Pet are seldom seen apart these days.

'What's up?' asks Dott. 'Have you decided to treat yourself to a new cuddly critter? Don't forget – a Bin Pet is for life!'

Clott picks up an extra-bouncy gold-coloured one and gives it a friendly squeeze. The delighted creature leaps on to Clott's back and snuggles in close.

'How about this little guy?' asks Clott. 'He's luv-er-ly!'

You remind Clott of your mission. You can't afford to get sidetracked – Bin Pets cost time and money! The disappointed Bin Weevil nods and puts the pet back in its pen.

'He is adorable,' agrees a small Bin Weevil with a pink bow in her antennae.

You immediately recognize Gosh, Posh's cute little cousin! Gosh is a sweet-natured youngster who's always smiling. As well as being Posh's number one fan, she is ker-azy about Bin Pets. In fact, she and Clott have got a lot in common.

You take Dott to one side and quickly tell her about Colin's predicament. Her face falls at the thought of the dragon roaming the Binscape, alone and unloved!

'I saw him just yesterday,' she sniffs. 'Gam came in

to buy some supplies. Colin's absolute favourite snack is a paw-ful of magic beans from the Giant Beanstalk, but Gam's bean harvest wasn't so good. Colin's tummy was starting to rumble!'

'Where did they go after that?' you ask.

'Hmm . . .' muses Dott, 'I'm not sure. Colin was desperate for more of those beans! I suggested buzzing over to Tycoon Island. There's always a swanky Bin Tycoon over there with more magic beans than they need.'

You, Tink and Clott weigh up your options. There's not much to go on, but this is the only lead you've got. That's when a manicured finger taps you on the shoulder.

'How frightful!' screeches Posh. 'I don't know what I'd do if anything happened to *my* little darling.'

'Me too,' says Gosh earnestly. 'Lady Wawa is the best!'

Your heart sinks. Posh, Gosh and the rest of the store have all been listening! You think of Trigg and feel rather relieved that he's on his way back to the mission control room – the SWS would not be impressed. Oops!

For once Tink makes a surprisingly sensible statement.

'There's no point worrying about what Bin Weevil knows what,' he announces. 'We've got to get on Colin's tail!'

Is Colin bonkers for beans? If you decide to scoot over to Tycoon Island, go to page 43.
If you rather fancy climbing the Giant Beanstalk, go to page 85.

Tink and Clott cover their eyes, but you're not budging. You stand on your tippy-toes and look the beast in the eye.

'Now hold on one roly-mo!' you say firmly. 'We don't want any trouble. We're looking for a dragon just like you.'

Magically, marvellously, miraculously, your words have an effect! The dragon opens his jaw wide, but no blast of fire comes out – just a series of strange squeaks!

Right on cue, another shape bounds up from behind Flum's Fountain. Colin! You watch entranced as Gam's beloved pet nuzzles the other dragon gently with his nose.

'They're identical!' you gasp.

'Not quite,' says Hunt, pointing to the stranger's tail. A single purple scale shimmers among the blaze of red and gold.

'They're practically twins,' coos Tink. His eyes suddenly cross, signalling one of his eureka moments!

'What is it?' you ask. 'Tell us, Tink!'

Tink recounts how Gam once told him about Colin's mysterious past. Gam rescued the reptile many years ago in the days of the Great Bin War. You're shocked to learn that Colin was one of *two* rainbow eggs, separated before they could hatch. Rumour has it that dark forces swiped the other egg.

You run over to give Rupert a hug. So colossal is the creature that one claw is all you're able to grip.

'We don't know how you managed to escape the wicked clutches of the WEB,' you laugh, 'but we're very glad you did!'

As you all head back to give Gam the good news, your chest puffs with pride. Dragon-hunting beats hat-shopping any day of the week!

The End

You, Tink, Clott and Gam troop solemnly across the Binscape, wondering what you're going to find out next. Today's revelations have been gobsmackingly shock-tastic already!

It's easy to spot the Garden Inspector's home – it's the brightest nest in the Binscape. Dancing Daisies sway merrily in the garden and Bubble Mushrooms cluster along the path. You're tempted to stop and smell the Venus Flytraps, but Tink has the sense to drag you up to the front door.

Ding-dong!

A meek face peeps out to greet you. It's not the Garden Inspector – she's hardly ever indoors – it's Sink, the mysterious submarine captain! Without her hat on, the poor creature looks rather sad and small. She salutes Gam, then hangs her head wearily.

'I am sorry,' she gulps. 'I didn't mean to disobey orders.'

Gam nods patiently as Sink explains her chance encounter with Colin earlier this morning.

'I was taking the diary back to the sub, sir,' she admits, 'when I bumped straight into your Colin! He was so thrilled that I picked up his stick for him, he ran up to say hello. I don't know what came over me then . . .'

There is a long, awkward silence. Gam takes a deep breath and clears his throat.

'Let me guess,' he begins quietly. 'You did what I should have done years ago. You opened the diary. You told Colin about his past.'

Sink nods her head.

'Do you want to see him?' she asks. 'He's having a think in the garden.'

You follow the agent up the garden pipe and out to the oasis outside. The Garden Inspector's patch is just as dazzling as you always thought it would be! Her green fingers have filled the lawn with terrific trees, crazy cactuses and brilliant blooms in every colour of the rainbow. There, on the other side of the pristine picket fence, sits Colin, his nose sniffing the scent of some Cat Flowers. The Garden Inspector steps out from behind a shrub and gives you a friendly wave.

'Don't worry about Colin,' she smiles. 'I've been singing to him. La, la, la, LAAAA! It always helps my plants – no reason why it shouldn't work for dragons too.'

Gam stretches up and gives his pal a pat on the nostril to say sorry. Colin's heart-shaped puff of smoke provides the response Gam was hoping for – the SWS leader has been instantly forgiven!

You cough politely before interrupting.

'Permission to start a new mission, sir,' you declare. 'Why don't we help Colin find his long-lost brother? Rupert's got to be out in the Binscape somewhere.'

Gam slaps you on the back, Tink and Clott cheer, and Sink stands to attention.

'Good work, Agent,' nods the SWS chief. 'Permission granted!'

The End

Clott's proposal certainly sounds appealing, but your antennae are telling you to head down into the gloom of the Castle Gam dungeons. The murky corridors are not for the faint-hearted, but you didn't sign up to the SWS for nothing! (Come to think of it, you can't exactly remember why you *did* sign up to the SWS, but at this precise moment you've got more important things to worry about.) While Gam's busy above ground, his dragon prowls every inch of those lonely tunnels, warming up the corridors with his fiery breath. If Colin were in trouble, you're sure that the slime-splattered castle vaults would be his first port of call.

'This way, Bin Boys,' you bellow, charging across Castle Gam's drawbridge. 'We're going underground.'

Tink and Clott dodge the giant spoon catapults that surround the castle, squinting up at the building's threatening silhouette. The place oozes mystery – touch the wrong stone and you could find yourself being charged by who knows what! It's a spookily spook-tastic location, making it the perfect hunting ground for dragons.

The three of you summon up your courage and step into the castle's ancient hallway. Candles flicker from wrought iron chandeliers and CCTV cameras coolly scan your every move.

'Look!' says Tink, pointing to a row of dark splotches dotted across the Castle Gam welcome rug.

Clott sniffs in disgust.

'Gam really should brush up on his housework,' he tuts. 'This carpet is filthy!'

'This isn't the time to swap vacuuming tips,' you snap, stumbling over to peer at the stains. Suddenly your jaw drops. Those splotches aren't stains at all – they're dirty dragon footprints! You gingerly prod a print with your finger.

'The mud is still wet!' you gasp, following the splotches into the gloom.

'Bin-tastic!' cheers Tink. 'Colin must have come home after a walk in the grime. He's probably sitting in the SWS control room with Gam right now, munching on a mitt-ful of magic beans!'

'No need for us to snoop about here then,' grins Clott, making a break for the castle drawbridge.

You grab your friend around the tummy in the nick of time. It's too early for congratulations and a shopping spree at Hem's – Colin hasn't been found yet! Besides, something doesn't feel right about the castle today . . .

That's when it hits you smack in the chops. Castle Gam is shiveringly cold!

'Colin isn't close by,' you decide. 'The place is freezing! He uses his fire to heat up the castle. Colin can't have been around these corridors for hours.'

'So who left those prints?' Tink wonders out loud.

There's only one way to find out! You, Tink and Clott follow the messy footprints down towards the dungeons. Soon the splotches get mingled in with the puddles that line the gloomy corridors. Gam's guards watch silently from behind their armour as the three of you troop grimly past, dodging drips from the leaky pipes and icky jets of slime. You don't bother to ask them for help – everyone knows that would be hopeless. Gam must have a hundred guards patrolling these creepy corridors, but you've never seen one engage anybody in conversation.

'Hey!' shouts Clott at the top of his lungs.

You, Tink and the nearest guard hastily shove your fingers in your ears – the echo down here is monumental!

'Is it a clue?' you whisper, tiptoeing over to take a look.

'Nah,' grins Clott. Instead the lucky Bin Weevil picks a shiny ten-Mulch coin off the floor and tucks it under his top hat. 'Maybe it's not so bad down here, after all!'

'A-hem!'

'Now what?' you ask. 'Found a bucketful of Dosh too?'

Clott gawps at you blankly.

'A-HEM!'

'That wasn't Clott,' insists Tink, tucking himself behind you. 'It came from in there!'

You lean in and listen again. Tink is right – someone or *something* is coughing loudly further down the tunnel!

'Choo! Sniff!'

You scratch your head. The noise sounds deeply unpleasant – like goo being squirted out of a hosepipe or an elderly Bin Weevil trying to swallow a chewy mouthful of Crushed Beetle Meringue. Whatever lurks ahead is not necessarily friendly! The corridor starts to narrow, before curving round a tight bend. Two tunnels lie before you – one to the right and one to the left. Which one will you choose?

If you select the right tunnel, go to page 63.
If your gut tells you to follow the one on the left, go to page 49.

You don't know what in the Binscape is going on up here, but it's more important than ever that you get Colin back to Castle Gam sharpish! You chuck the collar to the ground and then throw yourself over the edge of the Giant Beanstalk. Luckily Tink has speedy enough reactions to catch you by the legs. You'd been in such a rush, you'd forgotten about the two-mile drop to the Binscape below! Eek!

'Thanks, buddy!' you grin, clinging on to a fresh green beanstalk shoot. 'Guess I got a bit carried away.'

You promise Colin that you'll be back for him soon, then start your descent. Slowly but surely, you and your friends inch back down the strong stalk, helping each other through knotty vines and over slippery leaves. As soon as your six feet touch terra firma, you are off – skedaddling through the Binscape as fast as your legs will carry you.

You sprint over the drawbridge to Castle Gam in record time. On the way, you make a mental note to try out for the next World Weevil Games, then hurry into the SWS mission control room.

'Good work, Agents!' splutters a relieved Gam, when he hears the good news.

'We just need to persuade Colin to climb down,' you explain. 'We thought you might be able to help.'

Gam adjusts his tin hat, straightens his cape and fetches his walking stick.

'I'll be right there,' says the chief, flashing you a toothy grin. 'I'll just fetch Colin's squeaky teether toy. He'll come down for that, there's no doubt about it.'

Half an hour later you're still drumming your fingers on the desk in the SWS nerve centre.

'It's going to be dark soon,' you gulp. 'Colin will be worried.'

Tink sighs and shakes his head, reminding you that you can't rush an old Bin Weevil.

After sixty more minutes Gam finally appears at the doorway, only to discover that he needs the toilet!

'Won't be a jiffy!' he beams, shuffling off to the bathroom.

'But sir!' you cry. 'Colin needs us *now*.'

'You're quite right,' says Gam, thinking of his beloved dragon.

He tells you to go on ahead, and that he'll catch up with you at the Giant Beanstalk as soon as he can.

Where will your rescue lead you next? Flip to page 79 to find out!

You decide it's time to experiment with some delegation. You send Tink and Clott into the bushes to investigate the strange rustling while you stay behind to chat to Sip.

'Please come out,' you beg. 'I only want to ask a few questions about Colin.'

Luckily, Sip isn't exactly a tough nut to crack. The Bin Weevil sheepishly gets to her feet and confesses that she's done something dreadful.

'Colin wandered up here this morning,' she explains, 'so I sent him home! I thought I was doing the right thing, but then I heard from Bunty and Posh that he's still missing.'

You suck your teeth in surprise. News really does travel fast in the Binscape! Sip, meanwhile, is inconsolable.

'Why didn't I walk him back to Castle Gam?' blubs the broken Bin Weevil. 'Colin could be anywhere by now! You know how he loves exploring.'

You nod sympathetically. Where in the Binscape could that dragon have got to?

If you decide to call it quits and head for your nest, go to page 54.

If you insist on waiting with Sip, go to page 70.

Your heart tells you to go Giant Beanstalk-climbing, but your head says the smart Bin Weevil would mosey over to Tycoon Island.

'If the magic beans were thin on the ground yesterday,' you reason, 'why would Colin head straight back there again today?'

Dott nods her head enthusiastically.

'There's another thing,' she reminds you. 'Colin is petrified of heights! Whenever it's meal-time, he waits at the bottom of the beanstalk while Gam climbs up and harvests the magic beans as a treat to munch on each day.'

You, Tink and Clott point your antennae towards the door – Tycoon Island it is!

'Yoo-hoo!' calls a shrill voice from the back of the shop. 'I'm coming with you!'

Posh picks up her handbag, straightens her tiara, then daintily pops Lady Wawa under one arm. Gosh picks up her cuddly Bin Pet toy and trots along after her.

'I'm not sure about that,' you grimace. 'It could be dangerous.'

'Yeah,' adds Tink, 'This mission is for SWS agents only.'

You turn to Clott, hoping that he'll back you up. Of course, he does the opposite.

'The more the merrier,' he grins daftly, holding out an arm to her ladyship. Posh expertly steps past him and sashays through the door. She clearly isn't taking no for an answer.

'If there's an animal in trouble, then we're tagging along,' she says firmly. 'Aren't we, Lady Wawa?'

You duly troop across the Binscape, passing the gleaming skyscrapers of Tycoon Island. It's the ultimate destination – the place that wealthy Bin Tycoons escape to when they want to spend, spend, spend. Everything is super-exclusive and mega-expensive!

It takes longer than you'd hoped to crack on with your investigations, mostly because of Posh's constant chatter and teetering high heels. The Bin's most famous It-girl knows anyone who's anyone! She stops to talk fashion with her designer stylist, Tong, then strikes a pose so that Snappy can take her picture. She's just about to grant Scribbles an exclusive interview for *Weevil Weekly* magazine when you and the Bin Boys grab her arm and drag her away. That isn't going to find Colin! When you finally emerge on the rooftop of Tycoon Towers, the view is breathtaking. Dosh's gold-plated helicopter is parked on the helipad, glinting in the afternoon sunshine. Swanky restaurants chime with the sound of clinking glasses as smart shoppers parade up and down, secretly admiring their reflections in the windowpanes.

'There's Bunty!' squeals Posh, trotting over to dish out all the gossip on Colin's disappearance.

You and Tink roll your eyes. The secret's well and truly out now – Bunty's the biggest chatterbox in the Bin! She seems *very* interested to hear all about the mysterious circumstances of the possible dragon-nap. She's also got a juicy titbit for you.

'I shouldn't say anything, but . . .' begins Bunty,

signalling for you to gather round, 'I heard that Colin had been hanging out at the Slime Pool today.'

'Excellent!' cheer Tink and Clott. 'Let's go!'

You hold back your mates for a moment. Bunty means well, but how do you know she's got her story straight?

'Mem's just over there,' you say, pointing to an elderly Bin Weevil wearing a funny green bonnet. 'Why don't we ask her? She's friends with Gam. I'm sure she'd remember if he or Colin had been over this way.'

If you decide to try age before beauty, go to page 56.
If you're happy to trust Bunty's tale, go to page 74.

Within minutes you are standing outside the neon lights of the hottest nightspot in the Binscape.

'My favourite dudes!' beams Fling, boogieing down to meet you all. 'Fancy joining me for the Bin Weevil Wobble?'

The fun-loving Bin Weevil shimmies in time to the music, showing off his sharp white disco suit and swinging gold medallion. When he breaks into an impressive Bin-body-popping sequence you notice a large twig sticking out of his trouser suit collar.

'Why have you got a stick in your suit?' you ask, reaching over to tug it out.

Fling rubs his yellow neck and grins.

'Thanks!' he replies. 'That has been itching me ever since I put the bins out this morning. I thought it was the rhinestones on my collar. Not that I was going to change — a dude's got to suffer if he wants to look this good!'

You are still holding up the stick when Colin suddenly bounds round the corner, swishing his tail like an over-excited puppy!

You and your friends grin at each other — so that's why Colin set off for the club at top speed. Gam must have thrown Colin's toy further than he realized this morning — straight down the back of Fling's disco suit!

It's time to get Colin back where he belongs. If you hurry, you can pick up your new crown and get back for a boogie at the nightclub. Nice move!

The End

You don't stop to ask any more questions – how can you? The imperative is to fly to Mulch Island and track down the mysterious submarine captain – like . . . yesterday! The way you see it, that fleeting glimpse of Sink on the mainland is the best lead you've had so far. Before Tink and Clott can even check their passports, the three of you are boarding a plane at Rum's Airport. It's just a short bumpy ride to Mulch Island – the most exotic place in the Binscape!

'Let's split up,' you suggest, feeling the sand between your toes. 'Clott! I need you to look out to sea to try to spot a submarine periscope. Tink! You should head into the jungle – Sink might still be on the island stocking up on supplies. I'll walk along the shore and see what I can find here.'

You and your Bin Buddies bump fists, agreeing to meet later. For now at least, you're on your own.

'Let's start over here,' you decide, heading past Tink's Blocks towards the parasols dotting the sand.

You spend the next hour patrolling the beach, searching for clues. You'd still be at it now if the sun wasn't so scorchingly hot. You try your hardest, but the delicious sight of the Ice Cream Machine is too good to resist. Before you know it you're up to your antennae in a scrummy cone of strawberry ice cream. The taste is so good, it's criminal! Your mission has reached meltdown, but for now at least this SWS agent has chosen to chill.

The End

'OK,' you finally blurt out. 'Let's see it!'

Lab grins from ear to ear, then leads the way into his mind-boggling 8-Ball-shaped laboratory. The lab is a hive of activity today – potions bubble, computer screens beep and printers hum as they churn out baffling strings of numbers.

'Careful, Clott,' warns Lab, pointing to a purple test tube bubbling over a Bunsen burner. Lab is fascinated by the craziness of Clott's brain, but a spillage in here could cause a major explosion!

'Show us what you've got,' you say, keeping everything crossed.

Lab reaches under his counter and pulls out a robotic arm with a metal claw on the end.

'I call it the "Gizmo Grabber",' he says proudly, 'but you could use it to pick up Bin Pets too. Let me show you how to operate the remote control.'

You flash a stare at Tink and Clott. The Gizmo Grabber is never going to lift Colin all the way down to the ground!

'I don't think it's a goer,' you sigh.

Lab looks confused. 'Didn't you say you needed to rescue a Bin Pet stuck up a tree?'

'Make that a *dragon* stuck up a *Giant Beanstalk*,' you explain, feeling guilty you gave Lab the wrong end of the stick.

You exit the lab at your lowest ebb yet. You've wasted so much time that by now it's dark and the Binscape is black. A good night's sleep should sort you out, so you trudge back to your nest. You'll resume the hunt for the disappeared dragon at first light, keeping everything crossed until then.

The End

A tingly feeling in your belly tells you to take the tunnel on the left. Either the Slime Sandwich that you ate for breakfast is coming back to say hello or there's something interesting up ahead!

Tink and Clott tiptoe behind you, trembling silently as you step over puddles of goo and stoop under mildewed arches. With every intrepid step the echoes get noisier and noisier.

'What was that?' gulps Clott, as the tunnel rumbles with a deafening raspberry sound.

You shrug your shoulders and grimly push forward. If Colin *is* lurking in the dungeons, he's got a serious case of wind.

'AH-CHOOOO!'

Tink presses himself flat against the wall and starts to shake.

'It's just round this b-b-b-end!' he stutters.

'Bin-Weevil up, Agents!' you command. 'We're doing this for Gam and the SWS. Three, two, one . . . go!'

You bravely storm round the corner, ready to take on whatever lies in wait.

'Huh?'

Instead of a dangerous underground monster or even your old friend Colin, you find yourself nose-to-nose with Flem! Suddenly the weird noises make sense – those hacking howls and raucous raspberries must have been Flem coughing and blowing his nose! The sickly Bin Weevil has had a cold since *forever*, and being in a dank dungeon can only have made things worse.

'What are you doing here?' you ask, taking in the gloomy scene. Poor Flem has been tied to a pipe by his dressing-gown cord!

Tink and Clot quickly untie the Bin Weevil and help him to his feet. After five sneezes, a gargle and a phlegmy cough, Flem explains all.

'I'd just wandered into the Castle to visit Gam when I was bundled down to the dungeons!' he says breathlessly. 'Octeelia and her Thuggs are in the building. After they tied me up, the mob scuttled off in that direction. I don't know what creep-tastic evilness the WEB are up to, but it certainly isn't healthy. Ah-choo!'

You frown at your fellow agents. The situation is much worse than you thought! What has all this got to do with Flem? How could it be connected to Colin's disappearance? And when will these questions get some answers? Right now all you've managed to do is find somebody you didn't know was missing!

If you want to find out first-hand what Octeelia and
   her cronies are up to, go to page 12.
If you decide to get out of the dungeons and warn
   Gam, go to page 55.

'What shall we do, lads?' you ask, grasping Tink's arm and pointing to his invisible timepiece. 'If someone's nabbed Colin, they'll be making their getaway right now!'

The Boys from the Bin pace around in circles, rubbing their chins and staring off into the distance. Tink pulls a notebook out from his waistcoat pocket and starts to scribble thoughtfully. When Clott peers over his friend's shoulder, he looks impressed, nodding his head and pointing every time Tink scrawls something important. You and Trigg nervously stand and wait.

Five minutes later and you're both still waiting. Every time you try to interrupt Tink and Clott, however, they raise their hand to stop you getting too close.

'Shh!' whispers Clott, putting his finger to his lips. 'Tink's not finished yet!'

Trigg arches an eyebrow, but you insist on waiting a little longer. Somehow your Bin Buddies have managed to scrape their way through all sorts of risky SWS missions. As you watch Tink sketch, you assure Trigg that the pair will come up with a foolproof plan to find Colin.

After another ten minutes huddled under the billboard, though, curiosity finally gets the better of you.

'Oh, come on!' you cry, snatching the notebook from Tink's mitts. 'Show us the stinking plan!'

'Plan?'

Tink looks confused. You turn the book round to discover a daft sketch of Tink and Clott standing in front of Rott's Dump, waving their arms like loonies.

'Eh?' you yelp, flabbergasted. 'What's this got to do with Colin?'

'Nothing,' replies Tink. 'I just thought I'd draw a nice happy picture to cheer everyone up!'

'Told you,' mutters Trigg, rolling his eyes. 'A waste of time!'

'Well, *I* think it's jolly good,' replies Clott. 'The way Tink sketched the holes in Rott's string vest is weevily inspired.'

You mouth the words 'What are they like, eh?' at Trigg, then flash him an apologetic grin. While your pals coo over their doodles, you brace yourself for action.

'We'll start our search at Castle Gam,' you announce boldly, marching away from the Shopping Mall. 'We'll keep you posted, Trigg!'

'Wait for us, boss!' yell Tink and Clott, scurrying to catch up.

The three of you scamper across the Binscape as fast as your numerous legs will carry you. You figure that Colin's stomping ground has got to be a good place to start your search – the dragon has been guarding the Castle's eerie stone walls ever since he was first hatched! Before long, the foreboding fortress looms up before you.

'Let's head straight to the dungeons,' you decide. 'Colin spends most of his days down there.'

Clott gulps nervously.

'Or we could head to the mission control room,' he suggests helpfully. 'Gam might have some news. Those dungeons are *awfully* dark and gloomy . . .'

If Clott's idea sounds sensible, head to page 25.
If you're tough enough to dive into the dungeons, go to page 37.

'Let's go!' says Tink, pointing to the bright lights of Club Fling.

You nod absent-mindedly, but you're still not quite ready to turn your back on Flum's Fountain. Hunt has inspired you to scour the place for a few more clues. You tiptoe a few steps forward, studying the area through her super-duper magnifying glass.

'Look!' you gasp, pointing to the next marble column. 'More black marks!'

'There's one on the ground here too,' adds Clott, crawling through the dust.

You leap from smudge to smudge, your eyes glued to the magnifying glass. A few metres further on, you discover something really special.

'It's a . . . claw!' you cry.

Tink and Clott suddenly fall silent. Hunt coughs nervously.

'It is indeed a claw,' she whispers. 'A claw that is still attached to a very large dragon!'

You squint as the glass reveals the tip of the claw, leading to a large, scaly foot. Creeping catastrophes! You sheepishly pull yourself up to your full height. The creature does the same. Not only are you standing toe-to-toe to a dragon, it's a dragon that almost certainly is *not* Colin!

The dragon's flared nostrils, bared teeth and swishing tail all say one thing – he doesn't have a clue who you all are. It's a beast's basic instinct to bite first and ask questions later. You're in deep dragon doo-doo!

If you think it's a good time to run for your lives, rush over to page 15.

If you fancy trying your hand at dragon-taming, go to page 34.

53

You give Sip a hug, and persuade her that the missing-dragon fiasco is really not her fault. You have no choice but to call your pals back out of the bushes — you've run out of ideas!

'Colin is a smart cookie,' you shrug.

'He's a smart dragon, as well,' chips in Clott, trying his best to be helpful.

'I'm sorry, lads,' you confess. 'I don't think there's anything more I can do — Colin has eluded us. It's best that I scuttle back to my nest. I've flunked this mission with flying colours.'

Suddenly Tink begins to chuckle.

'Not quite . . .' he beams, before announcing, 'SURPRISE!'

Your jaw drops as Colin, Gam and a whole bunch of your favourite Bin Weevils leap out of the bushes. Even Sip leans over the counter and blows a party popper in your face!

'What's all this for?' you ask, as someone passes you a delicious Groovy Smoothie to slurp.

Gam wanders up and heartily shakes your hand.

'Your tireless commitment to the Secret Weevil Service has been noted,' he says proudly. 'We thought we'd reward you with a Slime Pool party.'

'And a little harmless prank,' admits Tink, mouthing the word 'sorry'.

Clott gives the signal for the musicians on the Jam Stand to start their tropical grooves.

What's an SWS agent do? It's time to part-ay! Colin gives you a friendly wink, then tilts his head towards the water slides. As far as you're concerned, that's an invitation . . .

The End

WEB agents randomly tying up innocent Bin Weevils? Octeelia and her crew marauding through the castle? You have no clue what the vile villains are up to, but you sense this is big – much bigger than you, Tink and Clott can hope to handle. You must report to Gam as soon as you can.

'This way, Agents!' you whisper, grabbing Flem's dressing-gown cord and leading him back down the tunnel through which you first arrived. If you can make it to the mission control room, perhaps Gam and Trigg can shed some light on the worrying turn of events.

You all scuttle through the slippery corridors as fast as you can. Getting back to ground level would be a cinch if only every tunnel didn't look exactly the same! You double-back, trace and retrace your steps, before ending up at the same slime-stained pipes where you first discovered Flem.

'Hi-yah!' A moustached figure lurches out of the shadows, flooring you with a karate chop to the back of the neck. Ouch!

You peer up into the gloom and see your old pal Kong Fu, the strongest member of the Secret Weevil Service! Kong Fu is responsible for training all new recruits. From martial arts to marksmanship, he's taught you everything you know. The second he recognizes you, his face breaks into a warm smile.

'I've been scouring the tunnels for clues,' he explains, spotting your companions. 'Hello, Agents Tink, Clott and . . . Flem? What are you doing here?'

But Flem's reply is cut short by a billowing ball of fire! Red flames lick the sides of the tunnel, reflecting your terrified faces in the pipework. Things are hotting up!

If you decide to run for cover, go to page 6.
If you're bold enough to stick around and face
    the flames, go to page 69.

'But the Slime Pool's so much fun!' groans Tink, desperate to leap into the pipe that heads to the coolest hangout in town.

All the hippest Bin Weevils like to chillax at the Slime Pool. There's gunk to slide into, happening tunes and the best smoothies ever sucked through a straw.

'I'll have a little word with Mem first,' you insist, 'then we might be able to slide down there for an Awesome Poursome or two.'

Tink and Clott reluctantly agree. Posh rolls her eyes.

'Well, I can't hang around on a rooftop all afternoon,' she sniffs. 'My antennae are being blown about all over the place! Lady Wawa, Gosh and I will slip over to the Smoothie Shack instead.'

Clott begins to argue but you quickly interrupt him, telling Posh that she's come up with a splendid idea. With the girls out the way, you SWS agents will be free to get stuck into some serious investigating!

As soon as the coast is clear, you stroll up to Mem.

'What's up?' you say casually. 'I'm guessing Gam has informed you that we're in a code red situation.'

Tink and Clott's jaws drop.

Mem doesn't even look you in the eye. There's no need – unlike your Bin Buddies she knows exactly what you're talking about! Although she appears to be a harmless old Bin Weevil, Mem has a very interesting part-time job – she's an occasional spy for the SWS! Mem has a photographic memory that is second to none, making her the perfect choice for stakeouts and observation work. As an SWS operative, she already knows about Colin's disturbing disappearance.

'I've been sat here since first light,' she mutters under her breath. 'You won't find Colin here. Haven't seen hide nor hair of him or Gam.'

You frown and kick the ground. You've reached another dead end!

'We've got nothing to go on,' you sigh. 'What are we going to do?'

'Did you see anything out of the ordinary, Mem?' asks Tink. 'Anything at all?'

The wise Bin Weevil tilts her head to one side so that she can think, her eyes as bright as a button. Just when you wonder if she's fallen asleep upright, she speaks.

'Two things,' she says mysteriously. 'I've heard strange noises in these parts. Squeaking sounds echoing across the tower blocks. Can't put my finger on what it might be. The other's even weirder . . .'

You strain your ears to listen.

'Something's going on at Dirt Valley,' reveals Mem. 'None of the flags are flying this afternoon.'

You thank Mem and press on, not sure what to make of her random revelations.

'Where to now?' asks Clott. 'Got any ideas?'

If you decide to zoom over to Dirt Valley, go to page 88.

If you think it's time to listen out for Mem's mysterious noises, go to page 89.

It's a dilemma. Push on with your mission or meet the fastest ever racer in the Bin? Actually it's not that much of a dilemma – this is *Ham* we're talking about! The racing ace is an all-time Weevil Wheels champ, with more trophies that he can fit in his nest. Of course you're going to go up and say hi.

You, Tink and Clott rush over to your hero, just as he takes off his super-flash red and white helmet. He gives you a beaming smile, then signs autographs for everyone.

You try to play it cool, but the sight of such a driving genius turns you into a quivering wreck.

'I don't want to be a pest or anything,' you snigger daftly. 'But what's it like seeing your name in lights above the track? Must be a total adrenalin buzz!'

Ham chuckles politely. He really couldn't be more nice! After letting you all take turns sitting in his car, he even drives you out for a time trial.

'That was wicked!' blasts Clott when you make it back to the garage.

Tink punches the air. 'You're the best, Ham!'

'OK, enough about me,' says Ham modestly. 'What about you guys? What do you do?'

You, Tink and Clott suddenly fall silent. You are, of course, fully trained signed-up SWS agents – not that you've even thought about your duties in the last few hours. It seems that this mission has gone into the pits. Try harder next time, Bin Weevil!

The End

You scratch your head and try to think logically. What would the WEB creeps be doing up the Giant Beanstalk and why would they be carrying a dragon-sized collar? You count off the evil agents that Octeelia has working for her – you have never seen Weevil X and the legion of Thuggs skulking around the Binscape with a dragon in tow. This sitch requires more investigation!

Tink and Clott stare at you forlornly.

'What about Colin?' they blub. 'Gam's worried about him!'

'Gam would understand if we delay things for a while,' you snap. Keeping the Binscape safe from the WEB is the Secret Weevil Service's top priority!

All this talk of Gam and his dragon has got you thinking. If the collar is about Colin's size, maybe it was meant *for Colin*! Now you're convinced that Octeelia has played a part in the reptile's disappearance. With his razor-sharp teeth, flicking tail and fiery breath, Colin would be an asset to any fighting force – good or evil.

'That spiteful spider has tried to steal Colin from under Gam's nose,' you bellow. 'Follow me, Agents! Colin had better come too.'

One by one, you creep back to the place where you discovered the mysterious collar. A jumbled row of footprints have pushed down the sprouting leaves, creating a pathway that winds all the way round to the back of Fum's castle in the clouds. You boldly stick your head round the stonework.

'Colin?' you gasp, doing a hasty double-take.

There, lurking in the shadow of the battlements, is another dragon, exactly the same size, shape and colour as Gam's pet pal!

Clott gulps. Colin snorts in surprise, releasing a jet of fire that lightly sears your weevily behind!

Tink stands still for what seems like ages with his eyes snapped shut. You suddenly realize that your goofy Bin Buddy is trying to think.

'What is it, Tink?' you demand.

'I know that dragon,' he replies. 'He's called Richard . . . Robin . . . no – Rupert!'

You, Clott and Colin listen open-mouthed as your friend hurriedly explains that when Gam first rescued Colin many years ago, he was one of two dragon eggs. The other egg contained Rupert – Colin's long-lost twin! Over the years, stories circulated that poor Rupert had fallen into the hands of Octeelia.

A horrible, eight-legged shape scuttles out from behind Colin's brother. Those stories were definitely true! Octeelia stands before you, her eyes shining with greed.

'My plan worked!' she cackles. 'Now I'll have two dragons for twice the destruction!'

Rupert tries to roar at his mistress, but a rather weedy squeak comes out instead.

'Shut it!' she sneers. 'Let's hope that Colin proves to be a better servant than you. What use is a dragon that can't breathe fire?'

Octeelia is a terrible opponent, but she needs to be stopped!

'So it was you who lured Colin away from Gam?' you challenge.

The arachnid cackles proudly.

'It was too easy!' she sneers. 'I used magic beans to tempt him all the way up the Giant Beanstalk. I knew that he'd be too scared to climb back down on his own. Now Rupert and I can drag him home at our leisure.'

Suddenly a scorching blast of fire roars past your shoulder. Colin has got something to say about this! Before you can say 'Spiteful spiders stink!', the furious dragon has driven Octeelia over the edge of the beanstalk! You crane your heads over to hear a faraway cry of 'I'll get youuuu!'

Suddenly Rupert takes to the sky. He may not be able to breathe fire, but his flying is first-class.

'Oh no,' you whisper. 'He's going to help Octeelia!'

Rupert loops round the castle one last time, but then drops down next to Colin.

'Don't worry,' smiles Tink. 'He's just checking she's gone!'

For now at least, you think, but know that the wicked WEB leader won't lie low for long. You had better go fetch Gam, you decide. It looks like the SWS leader is going to have two dragons to look after from now on. Bin-tastic!

The End

Your head flicks left, then right, then left again, taking in the baffling sight of the double dragons. Both have Colin's flaming red neck, knobbly back spines and pointy chin spurs. There's just one teensy thing that's bugging you . . .

'Have you ever seen Colin fly?' you ask your Bin Buddies.

Tink and Clott pause to think for a moment, then shake their heads furiously.

'Never!' gulps Tink. 'That's why Gam's always taking him out for walkies.'

'There's a good reason for that,' chips in Clott. 'Colin's petrified of heights. There's no way you'd see Gam's dragon looping the loop all over the castle!'

You all give yourselves a pat on the back, then make a dash towards Octeelia and her henchmen. You're within a Bin Weevil's whisker of reaching them too when Colin's lookie-likie soars through the sky and plucks you from the ground.

'Well, this dragon's certainly not shy!' you holler.

You, Tink and Clott hug each other for comfort, your legs dangling in mid-air.

Not only have you all failed to rescue Colin, you've managed to get yourself Bin-napped by his scary nemesis! As you soar helplessly above the Binscape, the shiny skyscrapers of Tycoon Island gleam in the sunshine below. Somehow you don't think you'll be dropping into Hem's Hats any time soon . . .

The End

You take your chance and bolt down the right-hand tunnel, sloshing forward through the gloop. The light is so dim you can barely see more than a metre in front of your weevily nose.

'Let's hold hands,' you suggest to Tink and Clott. 'We don't want to get split up down here!'

The three of you quickly form a SWS-agent chain. You boldly take the lead, groping your way along the dank stonework. The tunnel twists and turns like a maze, leading you left, then right, then back again. You never waver in your mission. With every new turn, the curious wheezing noise is getting louder and louder.

'A-HEM! SNIFF!'

That's when you finally see them. Two enormous murky shapes fill the underground chamber. You squint in disbelief. The shapes both have spiny backs, scaly skin and claws that glint fearsomely in the half-light. It's Colin and . . . a lookie-likie, dragony friend!

'What's up, big guy?' you ask, rushing over to give Gam's buddy a friendly scratch between the ears. The critter next to him shifts awkwardly in the tunnel, flashing a tiny purple scale at the end of his tail.

Tink and Clott gawp at each other in amazement.

'Rupert?' stutters Clott. 'It can't be. Can it?'

The dragon looks to the floor and shyly nods its head.

The Bin Boys explain breathlessly that this stranger is not a stranger at all – it's Colin's long-lost twin brother, Rupert! The pair hatched from rainbow eggs decades ago, in the dim days of the Great Bin War.

'I didn't know Colin had a brother!' you gasp. 'Where has he been all these years?'

'Gam rescued Colin before he was hatched, raising him as his own,' explains Tink. 'But poor Rupert fell into enemy hands. Last thing we heard, Octeelia and her evil mob had him chained up in their lair.'

'Not that the dragon was much use to her,' grins Clott. 'The word in the 'Scape is that Rupert can't breathe fire.'

Your antennae tremble with excitement. Colin's sudden disappearance, the muddy carpet and spooky noises all make sense now. Rupert must have escaped from the WEB and come to find his brother!

'Good work, Colin,' you say, impressed. 'Hiding Rupert in the dungeons was a top move. And what better way to while away the time than a fire-breathing tutorial?'

Colin nods, flaring his nostrils at the troubled twin. Rupert bares his impressive fangs, draws a deep breath, then takes aim at a torch fixed on the far wall. 'Choooo!'

Oh dear. Instead of setting the torch alight, the poor creature splatters the wall with a nose-ful of dragon snot! Ew!

Rupert groans in despair. This master class is getting nowhere fast! It is certainly a problem – no dragon worth his smoke would be seen out in the Binscape without a proud pair of flaming nostrils!

Luckily you have the ideal solution. You think back to your encounter at the Garden Shop.

'We need to get over to Trigg's place,' you suggest. 'One sniff of his Leopard Chilli Vine is guaranteed to get Rupert breathing fire! It's spicy enough to put hairs on his chest too!'

Tink and Clott high-five wildly. You set off, congratulating yourselves on how clever you've been. The movies can wait. To the Leopard Chilli Vine – and quick!

The End

You always have a fascinating
time at Lab's place, but you really
have got to be somewhere
super-urgently. Besides, you've
had some dicey encounters with
some of the Bin Weevil's wackier
inventions. His Venus Flytrap
Wrangler turned on you when you
were doing the watering and you've
lost more gear than you care to
remember in his Black Hole in
a Box.

'Can't stop,' you shout over
your shoulder. 'Got to get to
Colin!'

Before Lab can argue, you
are skidding back across the Binscape, then climbing the
beanstalk, six legs at a time.

'Colin!' you call anxiously. 'Are you still there?'

No, it appears, Colin is not.

Tink and Clott scamper over to the dragon's hiding place.
All that is left are a few charred magic beans.

'That collar's disappeared too,' gasps Tink.

'Oh help!' cried Clott. 'I don't like the sound of this . . .'

Your chest starts to thump. You peer up at the castle and
notice that Fum is still snoring soundly. Who could have crept
up here and taken Colin from underneath the sleeping giant's
nose?

A cackle echoes across the castle ramparts, sending an
icy chill up your legs, straight into your heart.

'Octeelia!'

You turn to face the evil mastermind. The devious

arachnid scuttles forward, clutching a length of her steely web. You, Tink and Clott gulp at the sight of Colin attached to the other end, wearing the black and red collar!

'Give our dragon back!' you shout, lunging for Colin's lead. Octeelia uses her split-second timing to slip out of reach.

'It's not yours any more!' she shrieks. 'This reptile is a servant of the WEB! Scuttle off now and tell your ridiculous leader. I'm sure Gam will be keen to hear what a bungle you've made of this mission.'

Your cheeks flush scarlet. Tink and Clott's turn a similar shade too. A silly error of judgement has cost the dragon his freedom! How will you ever redeem yourself?

When you are at your rockiest bottom, sometimes (just sometimes) inspiration strikes. You still don't really know what made you pluck the magic bean from the stalk and hurl it towards Octeelia, who instinctively caught it. All you do know is that watching Colin snap up the snack – Octeelia and all – was the best thing you'd seen in ages.

The vile villain wasn't seen for a long time after that. Would you want to go out in public after going through the digestive system of a dragon?

The End

You, Tink and Clott try to soothe Colin as best as you can, but the poor creature is trembling from teeth to tail. Every time you try to lead him towards the edge of the Giant Beanstalk, the dragon breathes a jet of fire, warning you to stop.

'So *that's* why he never flies,' concludes Clott, helpfully. 'Heights totally freak him out!'

You nod. That also explains why Gam climbs up the beanstalk every day to come foraging for magic beans. Colin must have been starving to have attempted this by himself! You can't help but feel sorry for the creeped-out creature.

'Aw!' moans Tink. 'He's got to come down. A dragon can't live up here forever!'

You remind your pal of Dott's advice. Every animal needs to be treated with love and patience if you want to get them to do the stuff you want them to do! After another half an hour of coaxing, however, you're running out of ideas.

'It's time to bring in the big guy,' you decide. 'Let's head back down to the Bin. We need to fetch Gam.'

Clott tickles Colin's chin.

'Maybe your master will be able to get you down in one piece,' he says kindly. 'Stay here, Colin.'

The dragon curls his tail around himself, then puffs out a smoke ring. He's not going anywhere – that's the whole point!

You, Tink and Clott are just about to slide down the nearest green shoot, when . . .

'Snnnoorrre!'

Fum lets out a rumble so thunderous that you are all thrown to the ground! The Giant Beanstalk wobbles and shakes as the dozy giant turns over, before nodding back into a deep, peaceful sleep.

67

'What's this?' you cry, scrabbling back to your feet.

There on the ground is a black and red collar, emblazoned with the letters 'W-E-B'! You pick it up and examine the collar carefully.

'Don't touch that!' stutters Tink. 'Look at the letters! That's got to belong to the Weevil Extermination Bureau. Octeelia and her Thuggs are out to get us!'

Clott jumps into Tink's arms and starts to suck his thumb.

'I want my mummy!' blubs Clott.

'They're a horrible bunch,' Tink adds.

You've got to admit, this isn't Bin-tastic news, but there's no point in panicking. You look at the collar again. It's big. Big enough, in fact, to fit a dragon about Colin's size!

If you decide to press on and fetch Gam, go to
     page 40.
If you've got the courage to check out what the
     WEB are up to, go to page 59.

'Not that way, *this* way!' a voice screeches.

You should really run, but your feet say otherwise. You, Tink, Clot, Flem and Kong Fu stand firm as Octeelia and her henchmen swarm into the tunnel, her arms wrapped around Colin's neck. The dragon keeps trying to buck her off, but the cunning spider has tethered herself to him with her web.

'Stop!' you bellow, waving your hands in desperation.

At the sight of your friendly faces, poor Colin snuffs out his flames and skids to a stop before you.

'This dragon belongs to Gam!' barks Kong Fu. 'Let him go.'

Octeelia throws her evil head back and laughs.

'He's *my* dragon now,' she snaps. 'And I won't be giving him back any time soon. So long, suckers!'

She points forward, but Colin canters back in the opposite direction. Octeelia looks ready to explode.

'Don't start this again,' she spits. 'We've been stuck in these tunnels for hours. Move it!'

You flash Colin a secret smile – you've sussed his plan.

'Good luck, Octeelia,' you grin. 'There are hundreds of miles of dungeon under Castle Gam and this dragon likes to prowl every inch of them. Before long you'll be wondering whether you Bin-napped Colin or Colin Bin-napped you!'

Octeelia's mouth twitches. Perhaps pinching a dragon wasn't one of her better ideas. The evil creature has trapped herself in a web of her own making! Before you can say 'Fall in and flip out!' the vile villain slides down from Colin's back and scuttles off into the shadows.

The good times are back – for now, at least!

'Come on, lads,' you say to Tink and Clott. 'We've got a movie to catch!'

The End

You do everything you can to calm Sip down – the poor Shack owner has worked herself into a weevily bad state. Once she's blown her nose, cried on your shoulder and collapsed on the counter, you try to pick up the conversation.

'What sort of mood was Colin in when you saw him today?' you ask.

'You know what dragons are like,' replies Sip. 'Playful as usual! Colin loves chasing things and running around as fast as he can. Normally he just scampers up to say hello, wags his tail and runs back to join Gam at Flum's Fountain.'

You take a long, thoughtful sip of your smoothie. What was different about today? Why didn't Colin bring his stick back to his master like he always did?

You sip again, thinking so hard you get brain-freeze. The Smoothie Shack is a cool place to hang out if you're thirsty, but not so good if you've got a difficult case to crack.

'Ah . . . so that's where it went!'

You lift up your head to see Tink and Clott pointing up at the Smoothie Shack roof, closely followed by Colin!

You all rush over and each hug a huge dragon claw tightly.

'Where did you get to?' asks Sip. 'We've been so worried.'

Colin looks wide-eyed.

'I can answer that one easily enough,' pipes up Tink. 'He's been here all the time! Look up there on the roof – Colin's stick has got wedged in it!'

Sip gasps in surprise.

'You mean that he's been here all day, hiding in the bushes?'

Clott nods his head.

'Colin's been lying there, keeping his stick in sight,' he nods. 'Dragons get very attached to their playthings!'

Now that you've found the missing reptile, Sip serves

up another tray of smoothies . . . on the house! Your Bin
Buddies glug down one more umbrella-topped glass, then get
ready to return the dragon home to Castle Gam.

'Hang on one minute,' you insist, clambering on a stool.
'We mustn't forget Colin's stick!'

The End

You conga past the cool Bin Weevil statues, then bounce on the trampolines in the gloopy slime bath. It doesn't take long to jump up to the Jam Stand at the top of the resort.

From here, you can see right across the Slime Pool. Down below, Posh is showing off her pretty new parasol to a group of admiring Bin Tycoon girls, while Lady Wawa snuggles up under a palm tree. The place is totally exclusive, which makes you wonder what Colin might have been doing here. Gam's dragon would be more at home in a damp dungeon than stretched out on a sunbed.

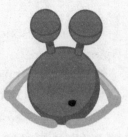

'There's Bongo!' shouts Tink, dancing up the Jam Stand. A happy-go-lucky musician grins and waves, serenading you with a funky drum solo. Bongo is the Bin Weevil who never misses a beat. He's so obsessed with rhythm he's been banned from Tum's Diner because he can't stop tapping the counter with spoons! Bongo's favourite hangout is the Jam Stand. Here he can play music to his heart's content. The Jam Stand's all about joining in – everybody can have a go! Tink grabs a pair of maracas and Clott tries tooting into a saxophone. You pick up a guitar and start strumming.

'Like it . . . !' beams Bongo, throwing down a few beats for you to follow.

You try some crazy new chords that somehow manage to sound p-r-e-t-t-y awesome!

'Hey,' nods Bongo. 'You're nearly as good as that dragon friend of yours.'

You're so taken aback, you drop your guitar in surprise.

'So Colin has been here?' you ask.

'Can I tell you a secret?' asks your musical mate, putting a finger to his lips.

You, Tink and Clott are amazed to learn that Colin has indeed been to the Jam Stand – in fact he goes there all the time! The reason? Bongo's been giving him secret guitar lessons!

'That dude has wanted to play an instrument since forever,' beams Bongo, 'so I agreed to help him out. Colin wants to perform at the castle one day. It's not easy playing with a tail and three claws, but Gam's dragon buddy gives it a good go!'

'So where's Colin now?' you wonder out loud.

'Hiding in the palm trees, practising his strumming,' replies Bongo.

You feel a flush of mischief tingling inside.

'Call him back,' you smile. 'It's time we had a dragon jam!'

The End

Tink and Clott pull a face. Waste time talking to an old Bin Weevil or jump straight into the Slime Pool to do some serious first-hand investigating? It's a no-Bin-brainer.

You give Mem a friendly wave, then follow your best buddies down the golden pipe that drops you at the hottest hangout on Tycoon Island. Posh, Gosh and Lady Wawa are already one step ahead of you!

As soon as you feel the warm breeze tickle your antennae and the sand between your toes, you can't help agreeing with the gang's decision. The Slime Pool is the best place ever! Bin Tycoons swish up and down, dressed in all the latest fashions, while chilled-out grooves pump all around. Daring Bin Weevils whizz down the water slides, landing in a squelch-tastic bath of slime. It's totally tropical!

The temptation to relax under a palm tree is nearly too much, but you know you ought to make some enquiries about Colin.

'Let's start our "enquiries" at the Smoothie Shack,' suggests Tink, licking his lips in anticipation.

'Wait! There's a new crew setting up at the Jam Stand,' says Clott. 'We could ask them.'

If you think there's a scoop at the Shack, go to
    page 21.
If you're in the mood for music, go to page 72.

'Did you hear that?' you cry. 'There's something in the bushes.'

'I heard it!' pipes up Tink.

'Me too!' adds Clott.

Sip is crouched behind the Smoothie Shack counter, a tea towel over her antennae. She doesn't say a word. Just what is going on? You're determined to find out!

'I'm going to investigate,' you announce in your most official SWS-agent voice. You stride purposefully into the bushes and take a look around. Wowsers!

It's Colin, curled up in an unhappy-looking ball! You encourage the dejected dragon to his feet, then lead him back out to the Smoothie Shack.

As you get closer, Sip slowly stands up behind the counter. The dragon tries to puff a smoke ring, but a bogey-coloured icicle drops out of his nostril!

'Are you all right, Colin?' asks Tink.

To everyone's surprise, Sip bursts into tears.

'No, he's not,' she confesses, 'and it's all because of me!'

The dragon shakes his head loyally, his teeth chattering.

Sip tells you that Colin strayed up to the Shack, during his morning walkies. He was terribly hot from fetching his stick time and time again, so as a special treat, Sip mixed an Ice Sloshy to cool the poor pet down. The legendary drink was concocted by an old friend, Slosh, the eccentric inventor.

'It was far frostier than I'd figured,' she sobs, 'and now I've snuffed out Colin's fire completely!'

Luckily you have just the remedy. 'Let's go see Trigg,' you tell the dragon kindly. 'A nibble of his Leopard Chilli Vine will get your spark back in no time at all!'

Inspired!

The End

'The Track Builder garage is smoking,' cries Clott. 'We'd better get over there!'

Clott and his best pal, Tink, scuttle up and down the track, gabbling about hosepipes, fountains and buckets of water. It's only when they start flagging down racing cars that Ham tells them to put the brakes on.

'Take five, guys,' he chuckles. 'There's no fire in the Track Builder garage! That's just the mechanics testing out the turbo on my latest set of wheels. We're all good!'

Ham is so effortlessly cool sometimes, you can hardly believe he's for real . . .

'Can we see Colin now?' you ask politely.

'Of course,' beams Ham. 'He's round the back of Track Two. It's where I go to relax between races.'

You, Tink and Clott scuttle after the champ, your pulses pumping. You *hear* Colin before you see him.

A loud strumming sound echoes out of a shed at the back of the track. You peep in and discover the dragon strumming on a golden guitar! He is beaming from ear to ear.

'Colin!' cries Clott. 'What are you doing here?'

Ham confesses that he's to blame. When Colin scampered into the yard this morning, chasing after a stick, the driver couldn't resist throwing it for the creature.

'After an hour or so of playing, we bonded,' he grins. 'That's one special dragon!'

When it was time for Ham's race, Colin couldn't remember his way back to Gam's Castle. Instead he crept into the driver's shed and waited for his friend to return.

'That's when he took a fancy to my golden guitar,' adds Ham. 'I keep it hanging on the wall. I can't play a note yet, but I've got plans!'

Right on cue, Colin strums a tune for you. The critter isn't half bad!

'He's always wanted to play a musical instrument,' smiles Tink. 'Gam told me that.'

'Talking of Gam,' you add, 'we had better take Colin home.'

The dragon nods his head. He gently picks up the precious guitar in his jaws and gives it back to Ham.

'Any time you want to jam, pal,' grins Ham, 'just give me a call!'

You shyly put your hand up.

'Does that go for us too?' you ask nervously.

When the Ham nods, your day is complete. You may not have bought your diamond crown, but you've solved a dragon disappearance *and* made a new celebrity friend!

The End

'Let's move it!' you shout, leaping into action like an over-excited Bin Weevil. Hold on a minute, you *are* an over-excited Bin Weevil!

You station Clott on Colin-calming duties and then lead Tink to the tallest, spindliest branches of the Giant Beanstalk.

'The best magic beans are way up there,' you say dramatically, pointing into the clouds. 'We're going to need at least two handfuls to get Colin through this.'

Tink salutes enthusiastically.

'You can count on me, boss!' he chirrups. 'I'm a weevily good climber!'

Soon you and your Bin Buddy are hanging from the top branches of the Giant Beanstalk, plucking off the juiciest magic beans you can find. It's an awesome view – from here, you can see right across the Binscape. You're tempted to take a quick pic to send in to the next edition of *Weevil Weekly* magazine, but you think better of the idea. You don't want Gam to hear that you've been sightseeing on the job!

Once you've got enough beans, the hard part begins. You sprinkle a couple of the titbits just in front of Colin's nose and wait for him to gobble them up. The plan works a treat! The dragon slowly creeps forward, nibbling and crunching each enchanted snack. He's having too good a time to notice that he's slowly but surely inching back down to the ground.

At this rate you'll have the wayward dragon in his dungeon before sunset. Congratulations, Agent, you've reached a whole new level!

The End

You, Tink and Clott beetle back through the Binscape in a bid to get to the Giant Beanstalk as soon as you can. You're not quite sure how you're going to get Colin back down, but at least you can sit with him until Gam finally gets there.

You scoot past Flem Manor, then sigh wistfully as you spot the flashing lights of Rigg's Multiplex. This morning's plan of taking in a movie dressed in a smart new crown already feels like a distant memory!

Just as the base of the Giant Beanstalk looms into view, you notice an old friend madly waving hello.

'Greetings!' beams Lab, shoving a test tube into his pocket so that he can shake hands.

'Can't stop,' you say apologetically, 'Got to rescue a pet stuck up a tree!'

The Bin's brainiest scientist nods sympathetically, then suddenly his eyes light up!

'Come with me for a tick,' he insists. 'I've got an invention that could definitely help you with that.'

Tink grabs your arm, and even Clott pulls a face. You've all encountered Lab's inventions before. Can you really trust the Bin Weevil that invented the Black Hole in a Box to come up with a sensible solution to your problem?

'Um . . .' you mutter, wondering what in the Binscape's name to do.

If you decide to pop your head into Lab's Lab, go to page 48.

If you think it's smarter to keep on running, go to page 65.

It's a no-Bin-brainer. You resolve to hotfoot it out of Flum's Fountain and make your way to Flem Manor.

'What about Club Fling?' wonders Tink. 'Those dragon footprints could be heading there instead.'

'Nah,' you insist. 'Colin hates loud noises. Those giant party blowers and banging club tunes would scare him out of his scaly skin!'

'Don't forget the confetti cannon on the roof,' pipes up Clott. 'Freak-tastic!'

You wave farewell to Hunt, then trot along the winding track that leads to Flem Manor. The path is dusty — so dusty that you can't even begin to pick one footprint out from any other.

You quicken your step. If the dragon *didn't* go this way, you need to eliminate it from your investigations pretty darn quick! Before you know it, the three of you are making your way across the lawns in front of the grand house. Flem Manor is the go-to location for Bin culture. Arty-looking Bin Weevils flounce around the grounds reciting poetry in theatrical voices, while would-be painters adjust their berets and make sketches of the posh pile. It's all terribly creative and right now you haven't a clue what this could possibly have to do with Colin.

You peer up at the grand house as a shadow flits past an upstairs window. You blink and look again. The window is empty.

'Let's go inside,' you suggest.

You, Tink and Clott shuffle into the manor's posh entrance hall. The grand staircase stretches impressively before you and noble Bin Weevil statues make you feel horribly small. Normally you'd stick your head in the drawing room and give your brain a wordsearch workout, but today you don't even hesitate. You sprint up the stairs two at a time.

'Let's see who's in here!' you cry, throwing open the door to the library. You run straight up to the window. Where was the figure you spotted earlier?

'The place is empty,' sighs Tink, throwing himself down on one of the sofas.

You swish the curtains closed and open again, then give them a shake for good measure. Could you have imagined the shadow in the glass? You stare sadly down at the lawns outside, cursing yourself for wasting precious time.

'Sorry, boys,' you frown. 'Must have been a red herring.'

'Snort!'

You can't help feeling a little cross at your pals' reactions. Yes, you messed up, but there's no need to laugh.

'Snort!'

You spin round to give Tink and Clott a ticking-off.

'Now, listen here,' you say crossly. 'Stop being so mean.'

The Boys from the Bin stare back at you blankly. Tink is swinging on the ladder that leans up to the bookshelf, while Clott is flicking through a nest-decorating book. You all stand in silence as the laughing comes once again.

'Ha, ha! SNORT!'

Quick as a flash, you throw yourself to the ground and pull out the sniggering shape of Weevil X. The sneaky villain is Octeelia's second-in-command – a mysterious no-gooder with a talent for lock-picking, foul fibbing and dastardly disguises. The sight of three SWS agents soon wipes the smile off his face.

'Get off me!' yells the intruder, wriggling to break free from your grasp. Tink has grabbed the baddie round the belly while Clott is holding down his feet.

'What's this?' you cry, pulling a dusty hardback out of his mitts. 'You've got a whole lot of explaining to do.'

Weevil X groans as you open the front cover and read: *Dragon Taming for Beginners*. You punch the air – the WEB really *is* at the bottom of Colin's disappearance! Octeelia's grumpy henchman has no choice but to reveal the organization's plot to Bin-nap Gam's best buddy.

'We could have done some awesomely evil things with Colin's fire-power,' grumbles Weevil X. 'I just needed to get the beast trained.'

'Never going to happen, my friend,' grins Tink, shoving the villain outside. 'You've got two minutes to lead the way to *our* dragon.'

You smile proudly as the dejected bad guy leads you out the back of Flem Manor, where Colin has been hastily tied to a tree. The dragon is thrilled to see you, but is not half as chuffed as Gam is going to be when he hears that his mission has been successfully accomplished. Weevily well done, Bin Weevil!

The End

'Now listen here,' pleads Tink, trying to appeal to Octeelia's better nature, mistaken in the belief that she has one. 'Colin would love to continue his flame-throwing class, but he's got a job to do. We need him to fire up the castle heating again. Everyone upstairs is starting to get frostbite!'

'We've let you have Colin for a whole day,' agrees Clott. 'If you leave now, maybe we can turn a blind eye to what you and your "team" have been up to.'

Octeelia flashes an incredulous 'They cannot be serious!' smirk at her henchmen, then collapses into an evil peal of *mwah-ha-has*. You and your pals have got to face it – the vile spider definitely *doesn't* have a better nature to appeal to!

You reach down into your pocket and jingle your hat-fund coins. It's time to appeal to Octeelia's greedy side instead!

'I've got a proposition for you!' you bellow, stepping a little closer to Colin.

Octeelia's top lip curls into a snarl.

'You pest!' she sneers. 'What can you have that would possibly be of interest to me?'

'How about some cold, hard Dosh?' you counter. 'One hundred Dosh coins for each of the dragons, no questions asked?'

The spider is silent for a short time. She's interested in owning a fire-breathing dragon, but the whiff of money interests her a whole lot more.

The deal is struck in minutes. Octeelia and her henchmen disappear clutching your hard-earned savings in their greedy mitts, leaving you free to unchain Colin and Rupert. The delighted dragons flap their wings wildly in applause. A splurge at Hem's Hats is out of the question now, but who cares! Colin is free and you've got a dragon-tastic new friend!

The End

'We have to pass Club Fling on the way to Flem Manor,' you reason. 'No harm in trying there first.'

'Are you sure?' says Tink. 'Colin is scared of loud noises and some of Fling's disco tunes are seriously thumping!'

Clott nods his head. 'Colin definitely isn't a party dragon.'

Hunt digs her bright red welly boots into the mud, then stoops to examine the dragon-prints even more closely.

'These tracks are blurred round the edges,' she concludes. 'Hmm . . . he could have been dragged but it's more likely Colin bolted off to the club by himself!'

You and your Bin Buddies gasp. But why? Maybe a trip to Club Fling isn't so outrageous, after all.

'Can I have a go?' asks Clott, pointing to Hunt's magnifying glass. The obliging Bin Weevil hands it over straight away, thrilled to have someone to puzzle with.

Clott takes the glass and holds it up to his face.

'Wowsers!' marvels Tink, his jaw dropping in surprise. 'Your eye has just grown totally massive!'

'Give it here,' you groan. Your Bin Buddies are loyal, friendly and generous to a fault, but they're about as sharp as a marble sometimes!

You hold the glass up to the stone column behind you. Up close you can spot a random example of 'I ♥ Posh' graffiti, the odd slime stain and a mysterious streak of black.

'That's a burn mark,' gasps Hunt, looking over your shoulder. 'Colin's definitely been here – the evidence speaks for itself!'

If you think it's time to press on to Club Fling, go to page 46.

If you decide to look for more clues around Flum's Fountain, go to page 53.

It's time for some weevily hard decision-making! You remember all the reasons why you joined the Secret Weevil Service. You signed on the dotted line for action, excitement . . . oh, and of course the chance to wear dark shades and a slick black suit. Secret agents live for dilemmas like this!

All the Bin Weevils in the shop wait patiently for you to make your decision. After five minutes of 'eenie meenie' and three games of 'rock, paper, scissors', you're ready.

'We're going to climb the Giant Beanstalk,' you call out to whoever's listening. 'If Colin's got the munchies that's the first place he'd try. Tink! Clott! Let's go!'

Everyone looks very impressed as you sweep out of the store – you even get a round of applause!

Ten exhausting minutes later you and your agent pals are clambering up the tallest plant in the Binscape. The Giant Beanstalk twists and curves into the clouds, green tendrils swaying in the breeze.

'How much further?' pants Tink, clutching on to the vine.

Clott clings on to your foot and heaves himself up behind you.

'Hungry?' he grumbles. 'Colin must have been starving to drag himself all the way up here!'

It's certainly not a climb for the faint-hearted, but if Gam can still do it at his age, pulling this off should be a walk in the park! The plucky old soldier has to inch his way up this mighty stalk every day of the week.

When you finally make it to the top of the Giant Beanstalk, you're all ready for a lie-down. It seems, however, that someone else has got there first!

'Snnoorre! Snuffle! Snnoorre! Snuffle!'

It must be Fum, the giant Bin Weevil that snoozes

his days away in the castle at the top of the beanstalk. Not much is known about this dozing giant. He doesn't mean to be mysterious: Fum is simply never awake long enough to reveal anything about himself. Rumour has it that Fum was once a regular-sized Bin Weevil, just like you. It's said that Lab accidentally zapped him with a reverse shrink-ray during a bungled experiment, turning him into a giant!

'Listen!' whispers Tink, pointing towards Fum's Castle.

You strain your ears. Just below the rumble of snoring you can make out a chattering sound. You scuttle through the leaves and discover . . . Colin! The desperate dragon is alone and frightened, his teeth rattling noisily as he peers over the edge. You and your Bin Buddies rush over and give him a comforting stroke on the tip of his tail.

'He looks like he wants to get down,' says Clott, 'but he's scared stiff!'

That's when you remember – heights give Colin the collywobbles!

> If you decide to call on some weevily expert help, go to page 67.
> If you want to use magic beans to coax the dragon down, go to page 78.

You sit back in your chair and try to take in the facts. Gam has given you some serious food for thought. The SWS leader explains seriously that he summoned Sink on to the mainland to collect an old diary that he wanted hidden. The yellowed pages contain the story of how he first rescued Colin back in the days of the Great Bin War.

'Colin wasn't the only egg I saw during those dark times,' explains Gam gravely. 'There was another one, exactly the same, belonging to his twin. I tried to rescue it, but the enemy got there first.'

Tink's jaw drops in surprise.

'Do you mean to say that there could be another Colin out there somewhere?'

Gam nods his head.

'There *definitely* is,' he replies quietly, 'and his name is Rupert. The last I heard, the poor creature had fallen into the hands of Octeelia and her treacherous Thuggs. I should have told Colin about him, but I thought it would be too upsetting!'

The sorry soldier bursts into remorseful sobs, leaving you with some serious thinking to do. You go back to the tape, but neither Sink nor Colin appears on the screen again.

'What if the agent bumped into Colin this morning?' you suggest. 'Maybe the sight of him gave her second thoughts about hiding the diary away?'

'When Sink's on land she always stays with the Garden Inspector,' sniffs Gam. 'I think we should ask her.'

What secret is Sink keeping to herself? Turn to page 35 find out!

You weigh up your options, then make a super-snappy decision.

'Come on, lads!' you cry. 'Let's zoom over to Dirt Valley. Those flags need checking out. We might even get to see some racing action!'

Tink and Clott cheer. This idea sounds much better than skulking around the top of Tycoon Towers listening out for squeaky noises! The three of you skid round to the racetrack in record time, hoping for a glimpse of the missing dragon.

The three of you have always *lurved* Dirt Valley. When you want to race, this is your place! You and your mates have had some truly nail-biting head-to-heads on the track over the years and you always buy your ticket to the annual Weevil Wheels Championship. It's totally Bin-tastic!

As you wander into the compound, you have to take your hat off to Mem's observation skills. The red, yellow and green flags really have disappeared. Only three charred flagpoles remain.

'Are you thinking what I'm thinking?' grins Clott.

'Yes!' you reply. 'The flags have been burned. Maybe Colin isn't so far away, after all.'

'Er, no,' replies your flummoxed Bin Buddy. 'I'm thinking that Ham's standing just over there. Shall we shimmy over and say hello?'

'The Weevil Wheels champ?' blurts out Tink. 'Co-ol!'

If you decide to check out those scorched flagpoles first, go to page 23.
If you can't resist zipping over to say hi to your hero instead, go to page 58.

'Mate . . .' whispers Tink, as you sit yourself down on the other side of the rooftop. 'Is there a chance that Mem could be just a teensy bit bonkers?'

Clott agrees.

'What's the old gal really told us anyway?' he argues. 'Bunty said that she knew someone who knew someone who had *seen* Colin at the Slime Pool, not just heard a few strange squeaks! We could be having fun at the Smoothie Shack right now!'

'Stay on task, Bin Weevils,' you reply sternly.

Just then four or five smart-looking Tycoons in top hats scuttle over to Dosh's glistening helicopter and jump inside. You all hold your ears as the chopper blades whirl round and round, lifting the vehicle into the sky.

The helicopter circles the Binscape skyline, darting in and out of billboards and office blocks. The journey isn't far – the vehicle sets down on an apartment building opposite.

'Posh folk, eh?' shouts Tink. 'Why can't they just take the bus?'

'I've jumped further than that!' moans Clott.

'Hold on,' you cry, sticking your fingers back in your ears. 'Dosh's chopper is already on its way back again!'

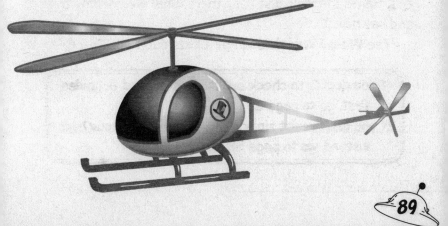

The golden helicopter makes an impressive sight as it soars towards Tycoon Towers. It's only when it gets a bit closer that you notice that the vehicle is bumping up and down at frightening speed. If it doesn't put the brakes on soon, it's going to overshoot the landing spot!

'That pilot had better watch out,' remarks Tink. 'Dosh will have a fit if he scratches that paintwork. It's 24-carat gold leaf!' You leap to your feet as the helicopter begins to dip and spin. It's almost as if it's hurling itself across the skies. You squint to try and make out who's inside the cockpit, but the vehicle has been fitted with tinted windows.

Each one of you is more than a little relieved when the wayward aircraft finally bumps on to its landing mark. The passenger door begins to rattle and shake. Someone must be desperate to get out!

'I don't think everyone enjoyed their flight,' you gasp, running up to get a closer look.

Who is going to clamber out of Dosh's helicopter?
Turn to page 18 to find out!